82990

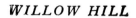

WILLOW HILL

Other books by
Phyllis A. Whitney

A Place for Ann
A Star for Ginny
A Window for Julie
The Silver Inkwell
Step to the Music
Linda's Homecoming
A Long Time Coming
The Highest Dream

PHYLLIS A. WHITNEY

Willow
Hill

David McKay Company, Inc.

New York

For My Daughter Georgia

Contents

x

CONTENTS

WILLOW HILL

NEWCOMER TO WILLOW HILL

Whenever there was a pause in dinner table conversation, Val glanced anxiously at the clock on the dining room wall. Plenty of time. The train from California wouldn't reach Willow Hill till after seven-thirty. More than an hour away and the minutes were dragging.

She tried to focus her attention on her mother's words and caught the familiar phrase, "Mrs. Manning says—" Across the table her father's eyes met hers and he winked in amusement. They had a private joke about Mrs. Manning.

Mrs. Coleman missed the wink because she was busy filling coffee cups as she talked. "Mrs. Manning says the meeting this evening is *so* important." Her neat small head with its softly waved brown hair nodded emphasis to that "so." "The Junior Auxiliary of young-marrieds is getting together and Mrs. Manning—".

"Well, let 'em get together without you," Mr. Coleman broke in. "You belong to the senior club—isn't that enough? All this committee stuff eats up your time as it is."

Val hooked her heels over the rungs of her chair. It was a habit forbidden since she'd been a little girl, but she had to hold onto something or explode. Junior Auxiliaries, senior clubs, meetings—when in just a little while that train would make the whistle stop at Willow Hill before going on to Chicago, and Stephen Reid would get off the train!

"Do you suppose he writes, too, like his father and mother?" The question popped out before Val could stop it.

"Who writes? Val, what *are* you talking about?" Mrs. Coleman asked.

"She's doing some hero-worshipping before the hero shows up," her father said.

Val sat up indignantly. "Why shouldn't I? All my life I've heard you talk about Douglas Reid and about what friends you were in college. Everybody says that before he died he was one of the best of all the foreign correspondents. And Margaret Reid has written real best-sellers. Even Mrs. Manning reads them. So why shouldn't I be excited when their son is coming to live in this house?"

"Of course, dear," Mrs. Coleman agreed absently, and Val suspected that her mother had not heard a word she'd said. She went on as if there had been no interruption from an excited daughter. "Mrs. Manning feels that this matter concerns the future of Willow Hill. If this housing project is allowed to open right on the edge of town, it's going to affect all of us unpleasantly."

Val sighed. When her pretty little mother really took the bit between her teeth, there was no managing her or distracting her attention. You might just as well settle down to admiring the way she looked and accept her current project.

Tonight she was especially attractive. She had skimped so long to buy that moss-green dress, but the result, Val had to admit, was worth it. She looked very smart and trim, and the new hair-do she'd tried was just right. It was too bad her daughter had not been able to follow a little more in her pattern, instead of being all angles and legs and hair that just hung.

Val glanced across the table at her father and was struck again by the contrast between her parents. Nick Coleman was no movie hero for looks. Mostly he was on the square side. Square shoulders, square jaw, gray eyes that as often as not had a twinkle in them. And he was a square-shooter, too. Clear through. But you wouldn't have expected anyone with Carolyn Coleman's neat, precise, tidy ways to have married a man who liked best to wear old slacks and a sloppy shirt, and who never managed to keep his hair smooth because he was forever running a hand through it the wrong way. But he was a good athletic coach and the kids at school were crazy about him.

Val looked at the clock again. Barely three minutes had passed. She tried to listen to what her father was saying.

"I don't see how your Mrs. Manning is going to stop that project from opening, Carrie," he said. "The houses are up and the first families will be moving in any day. The Hubbard Plant needs the men. It's a pretty big industrial proposition."

Mrs. Coleman looked vaguely troubled, but she clung to the words of her Woman's Club prophet. "Mrs. Manning says it isn't necessary for Hubbard to employ Negroes. And then to have this project at the foot of the hill—practically at the end of our own street! If you'd just take a little more interest in civic welfare—"

Nick Coleman passed his cup for more coffee. "One civic leader in a family is enough. Don't you think so, Val?"

Val nodded, but her attention had been caught by a sound outside. A car had pulled up to the curb before the house next door. There were voices, the slam of a car door, the sound of running feet.

"The Pipers are home!" Val cried. "Oh, mother—"

Mrs. Coleman shook her head gently. "Judy can wait, dear. Mrs. Piper won't want you underfoot right away. Do finish your dessert."

Bread pudding, Val thought disgustedly. When her best friend was home from vacation and there was this wonderful news about Stephen Reid to tell her! She took a mouthful of pudding and choked it down.

She could hear the two little Pipers, Binx and Debby, racing around the yard, while inside the house Mrs. Piper moved from room to room, flinging windows open with a businesslike bang. Mr. Piper could, as usual, be heard roaring objections to what all the other Pipers were doing. The family was behaving thoroughly in character and it was pleasant to have the long summer calm broken this first day of September in the familiar Piper manner.

There—that was Judy now, scolding Binx. If she could just get away from this table and over next door through the hole in the hedge. . . .

"Dishes first." Sometimes her mother seemed to read her mind. "Some of the senior group are meeting early and I'll have to leave in a few minutes. See that your father gets off in time to meet the train and be sure he puts on a tie. And tell Stephen Reid how sorry I am that I couldn't be home this evening."

Val nodded. "Yes, mother." Dishes! She simply *had* to get hold of Judy.

"And Val, honey," there was open distress in her mother's eyes, "do let's try to do something about your hair. It looks so—so limp. You really should take more interest in your ap-pearance, now that you're a graduating senior."

Val wound a soft brown strand around one finger and gave it a tug. She had tried everything she could think of with her hair and it always finished up in ends that just hung, so most of the time she tossed it out of her eyes and forgot about it. She hadn't been blessed with the sort of hair her mother had; hair that waved and fell into place at-tractively no matter what she did to it.

That she had managed one outstanding thing this summer in winning first place in a junior essay contest perhaps was some compensation for not being as beautiful as her mother. The Chicago newspaper which had sponsored the contest had printed her piece one Sunday in the literary section. Nick had practically burst off all his buttons and her mother had been truly proud and pleased. Perhaps they'd be equally proud if she could land the editorship of the *Willow Wand* this year.

Mrs. Coleman folded her napkin with a neat, quick ges-ture. "I'll have to dash. Val, will you run upstairs and get my club book and my white gloves? And don't forget, dear— dishes first. And everything in place before I come home."

Val ran upstairs to her mother's room. Even in her hurry she reacted with a mingled sense of admiration for this room and despair at her own inability to keep her possessions in such apple-pie order. The color scheme was cool blue and gray, with dashes of peach for warmth, and it was as femi-nine a room as Mrs. Coleman herself. The club book lay on its accustomed shelf, the gloves were in a drawer that breathed a flowery sachet when it was opened.

Imagine finding everything just where you'd expect it to

be, Val thought, and put the last glimpse she'd had of her own room out of her mind.

Her father had gone out to the rear terrace to smoke his pipe, and when Mrs. Coleman had left, Val rushed the dishes off the table and into sudsy water. She was half through washing them when she heard a familiar call.

"Oh, Va-al! Oh, Valerie-ee!"

Val put her nose against the kitchen window screen and hallooed a response. A moment later she heard Judy hailing Nick on the terrace. Mr. Coleman was "Nick" to the whole town, and even Val had picked up the habit of calling him by his first name as soon as she'd been able to talk. It seemed to fit him somehow.

Judy bounced into the kitchen, every red curl agleam, and enveloped Val in an unrestrained hug.

"Oh, Judy, it's good to have you home!" Val cried. "Look out for my soapy hands. Do I ever have news to tell you!"

Judy reached for a dry dishcloth and picked up a plate from the sink. "I know. Nick sent us the clipping. 'Willow Hill girl wins first place in essay contest entitled *What America Means to Me*.' May I congratulate the next editor of the *Willow Wand?*"

"Shush, Judy!" Val waved her friend into silence. "I *hope* it helps get me the editorship. But both Mary Evans and Sue Peters have worked awfully hard, and I fell down on some of those assignments Miss Kay gave me last term. I wouldn't blame her much if—"

"Don't be silly!" Judy was indignant. "After that America thing you've earned the right to top place."

"Anyway," Val said, "that wasn't what I meant by news.

This is *really* exciting. You know who Douglas Reid was, don't you? Nick's always talking about him."

"I guess so," Judy said.

"And his wife's a writer, too. She's the novelist, Margaret Reid. Mother had a letter from her."

Judy caught one of Mrs. Coleman's cups just in time as it teetered on the edge of the sink. Having rescued it, her quick-silver attention darted elsewhere. She went over to the rear window of the kitchen and looked out through the gathering dusk.

"What in the world? What are all those buildings at the foot of the hill? They weren't here when we went away at the beginning of summer."

"The foundations were in," Val said. "You just didn't notice. It's going to be a government housing project and the president of mother's club is trying to stir up the town about it. So Nick and I have been getting it served up at every meal. Judy, you're not listening."

Judy looked up from her investigation of a dish of peanuts. "Of course I'm listening. I'm fascinated."

"I doubt it. But anyway Mrs. Reid wrote us a letter. She wants to keep the Reid name in the newspaper field, so she's going abroad as a correspondent in Germany. And because Nick knew her husband so well, she's asked if we'd take their son Stephen until she comes home in six months or a year."

Judy looked mildly interested. "I hope he's older than Binx. I couldn't stand two at that age."

"He's going to graduate with us," Val told her. "He's just our age. Oh, Judy, I could shake you! Why do you have to be illiterate right now? Douglas and Margaret Reid are famous. Stephen belongs to a real writing family. And he's going to live *here*. He's coming tonight."

She glanced at the kitchen clock and began to dry her hands hastily. "I've been watching that thing all day, but the minute I turn my back it skips ahead. The train will be here in fifteen minutes. I'll have to get Nick off for the station."

She hurried out to the terrace with Judy in tow and then paused with her finger on her lips. In the hammock stretched between two posts lay Nick Coleman, his evening paper and his pipe on the ground beside him.

"He's asleep," Val whispered. "I hate to wake him up. He looked tired at dinner tonight. And school starts day after tomorrow. Coach Nick will have to be back on the job."

"Then don't wake him." Even in the dusk Val could see the conspirator's twinkle in Judy's eyes.

The two tiptoed back to the kitchen.

"Let's meet the train ourselves," Judy said. "We'd tag along anyway and your father'd probably be glad to have us take over."

Val hesitated. "I ought to powder my nose and do something about my hair."

"No time," Judy said. "We've lost five minutes already. Come on. We'll meet this Stephen Reid in person."

A few moments later they were walking briskly downhill. It had grown darker and street lamps were blinking on. The project houses looked empty and ghostly as they went by.

"If Stephen looks anything like the pictures I've seen of his father, he'll be super," Val said, putting into words the hope she couldn't express to anyone but Judy.

"Mm," said Judy, but she sounded so little impressed that Val glanced at her in surprise.

"What's on your mind?" she asked.

There was a suspicious twist to Judy's grin. "I have news, too. Wait till you hear who's coming over tomorrow to play tennis."

"Who?" Val asked, listening for the train whistle.

"Tony Millard." Judy tossed the name out airily and Val forgot the whistle.

"Tony Millard!"

"Come along," Judy said. "We're meeting a train. Remember?" But she was evidently pleased with the effect of her announcement.

"How, what, when and why?" Val demanded. "And tell me quickly."

"I thought I'd make you sit up," Judy said complacently. "After all, Stephen Reid is only somebody's son. But Tony Millard is the whole show at Willow High. Or hadn't you noticed?"

Val had noticed all right. You couldn't help but notice the boy who was class president, who ran away with all the track honors and played the best basketball in school. There wasn't a girl in their class who wouldn't practically swoon at the thought of dating him. And here he'd fallen to little Judy!

"How come he's yearning to play tennis with us?" Val asked.

"Not with *us*," said Judy modestly. "With *me*. The Millards were staying at the same resort and Tony and I sort of got acquainted."

Not only was Tony a big shot at school; his father was one

of the most important figures in Willow Hill. Once Wayne
Millard had made football history and his name still carried
an aura of glamor about it, though its owner was now head
of the Millard Real Estate Company and something of a
town father. Val remembered having seen him a number of
times—a big handsome man with an air of being able to run
successfully any enterprise that came his way.

"So Tony likes red hair," Val commented.

"Mm," said Judy. "Maybe." And then she dropped her
unnatural coyness and became her usual enthusiastic self.
"Oh, Val, do you think Tony Millard could really get interested in me? Wouldn't it be fun?"

"There's no reason why he shouldn't be interested in you,"
Val told her. "I don't know anyone nicer."

Judy slipped her hand through Val's arm and gave it a
squeeze. "I'll bet Stephen Reid will be special, too. How
could he help it with all those important ancestors? Then
maybe the four of us can run around together this coming
term. Maybe we can even make it doubles tomorrow."

Val hoped so. It would be wonderful to be included in a
foursome that boasted the presence of Tony Millard. And if
Stephen Reid *did* turn out to be special, and if he happened
to like her. . . .

They had almost reached the station. There was the Willow Hill sign and already the train's headlight was shining
down the tracks. They were still across the street when the
train came to a stop and a single passenger got off. He was
slight in build and not very tall and he had none of his
father's dashing good looks. He walked over to the bag a
porter had set on the platform and stood beside it, looking
uncertainly about as the train pulled away.

Val and Judy exchanged glances. There, thought Val, went the chance of teaming up with Judy and Tony Millard. Somehow Stephen Reid didn't look like the sort of fellow Tony would care much about.

"Oh, well," Judy whispered in comforting tones, "he does have an interesting background. Maybe he won't be so bad."

CHAPTER 2

STEVE

The two girls walked hesitantly across the platform toward the boy who stood waiting by his suitcase. Val spoke first. "You're Stephen Reid, aren't you?"

He had a nice smile, even if he lacked the build and looks of Tony Millard. "Right. And you're Valerie Coleman?"

Val nodded and introduced Judy, noting that while he was tall enough beside Judy, he topped her own height by barely an inch. Not that that was important really, she reminded herself. But she could not quite suppress a feeling of disappointment because Steve didn't fit the Tony pattern.

"Your father—" he said to Val, "is he—"

Val did not wait for him to finish. "We'd better confess right away. Nick was coming to meet you, but he went to sleep in the hammock after dinner and—"

"*We* wanted to meet you, so we didn't wake him up," Judy broke in.

"That was swell of you," Stephen said.

He picked up his bag and Val led the way from the platform to the sidewalk that wound uphill. They walked along in silence for a little while in the shadowy light thrown by street lamps through wavering branches.

"I'm looking forward to meeting your father," Stephen

said when the silence grew a little awkward because no one seemed to think of anything to say. "I've heard stories about him ever since I was a kid."

"My goodness!" Val said. "What kind of stories?"

"Oh, about how Nick was the sort of guy who never knew when he was licked. I guess my own dad caught something of that quality from him."

There was such sincere admiration in Stephen's tone that Val found herself listening in surprise. Everybody around town liked Nick, but she'd never heard anyone speak of him in quite that way before. Maybe you got to taking your own father so much for granted that it seemed strange to catch a glimpse of him through outside eyes.

But before Val could comment, Judy was making her own contribution to the conversation. "We're pretty proud of Val around here these days. You come from a writing family —maybe you'll be interested in hearing about her latest achievement."

Val wanted to pinch her. Dragging something like that in by its heels to make an impression on Stephen Reid!

"You mean that contest she won this summer?" Stephen asked. "I know all about that and I think she did an awfully good job of writing."

"How did you know?" Val asked in a small voice.

"Nick sent a clipping to mother. She liked the piece, too."

Val was surprised. Her father had been proud of her for winning the contest, but she hadn't dreamed that he'd gone to the trouble of mailing copies to the Pipers and the Reids. She felt a pleasant glow of pride over what he had done.

Judy gave a little skip as she walked along. "One thing I remember in your piece, Val—where you said something about America being nights like this, with tree-lined streets and friendly lamplight shining from the windows. I liked that."

"You're nice," Val said. "Both of you. But this is going to my head. It's a good thing we're nearly home."

The porch light flashed on just as they turned in the walk and Nick Coleman came hurrying down the steps to meet them. He'd forgotten about putting on a tie and his shirt was open at the throat.

"What do you two scamps mean by running off and letting me sleep when I had a train to meet? A conspiracy, that's what it is! Hello, Stephen."

He held out his hand and after that he didn't say anything for a minute, but just stood there gripping Stephen's hand and looking at him.

"Guess I don't look much like my father, do I?" Stephen said awkwardly and Val felt an unexpected tug of sympathy toward him. Maybe it wasn't too easy to be the son of two such important and handsome people.

Nick clapped his shoulder. "You look just the way Doug Reid's son ought to look. We're mighty glad to have you in this house. It's too bad Mrs. Coleman isn't here to tell you so herself, but she had something come up tonight that she couldn't help. She'll be along later."

Judy paused on the walk. "Do you play tennis, Stephen?" she asked.

"I get by," he said. "If you can find me a racket. But look —it's Steve. I keep looking around to find this Stephen guy every time you call me that."

"Okay, Steve," Judy said. "We'll make it doubles tomorrow and I'll hook Dad's racket for you. I've got to dash now. 'Bye, Val."

She vanished in the direction of the now invisible slit in the hedge and Nick led the way into the house.

"Maybe Steve would like to clean up a bit and have a look at his room," he suggested. "Suppose you take him upstairs, Val."

Val knew why her father didn't want to come up himself. He felt uneasy about Steve's room. He had wanted to fix it up for Steve in his own way, but Mrs. Coleman had had her own enthusiastic ideas on the subject. Both Nick and Val had tried gently to dissuade her, but she had worked so hard over it and been so pleased with the result that neither had had the heart to criticize.

Steve picked up his bag and followed Val upstairs. She pushed the door open with a sense of embarrassment. Not that the room was unattractive, but her mother *did* love things to be pretty. The result was a very feminine effort at what was supposed to be a masculine room. Val could imagine the snort of scorn with which Tony Millard would greet a room like this.

"Mother fixed it up," she said lamely. "Nick and I thought it ought to be—oh, plainer. But her heart was set on having it like this."

Steve stepped across the threshold and looked around. "It's a wonderful room. You don't know how good it makes me feel that you folks wanted to go to so much trouble."

Val released the breath she'd been holding. This Stephen Reid was going to be all right. He didn't mind the furbelows because he recognized the intention behind them. She could hardly wait to get downstairs and set Nick's mind at rest, but as she moved from the door, Steve looked up.

"Don't go," he said.

He had taken a big brown folder from his suitcase, and he opened it and set it up on the bureau.

"Your father and mother?" Val said.

There was affection in the look he turned on the picture. "I never feel moved in anywhere till I get that up."

Val came into the room for a better look at the pictured faces. There was courage in Douglas Reid's eyes and in the set of his chin, and in Margaret Reid's face were both strength and gentleness.

"They must be awfully hard to keep up with," Val said.

Steve nodded. "They are. But I guess you know what that's like with a guy like Nick for a father."

Val rearranged her thoughts with a start. Somehow she'd never worried much about trying to keep up with Nick.

When she went downstairs to tell her father that Stephen Reid didn't mind Mrs. Coleman's furbelows, she found herself looking at him with new eyes, trying to understand the way Steve saw him. It was queer how this boy whom she had known for barely a half hour was causing her to rearrange thoughts that had gone along in a rut for as long as she could remember.

Later, when Steve joined them downstairs, Val and Nick had time to show him about the house, introduce him to Nick's workshop in the basement and to the terrace overlooking the hill, before Mrs. Coleman came home.

She was back before they expected her, and Val, hearing the familiar click of her mother's heels on the front walk, hurried to the door to meet her.

Mrs. Coleman's eyes were bright with indignation and her cheeks were unusually pink. That meant something had gone wrong at the meeting, Val thought with a sigh. Not every girl had a mother who looked so pretty and young and she had been anxious to show her off to Stephen Reid. But if she was in a fluttered, worried state, that wouldn't be so good.

Her mother, however, neglected none of her duties as hostess. She managed to put aside her disturbing thoughts, whatever they were, in order to greet Stephen with words that were warm and friendly. And she was delighted when he told her how much he liked the room she had prepared for him.

"We'll have coffee and cake out on the terrace," Mrs. Coleman suggested. "Would you like that, Stephen? You must be terribly hungry after that long ride on the train. You men go on outside. It's a beautiful night—too nice to stay indoors. Val and I will be out in a jiffy."

In the kitchen she was quick and neat in all her movements, while Val managed to spill coffee over the brim of a cup, and smear frosting in cutting the cake. But Mrs. Coleman was busy with her own troubled thoughts and allowed her daughter's clumsiness to go unreproved. Val repaired the damage as best she could and walked with unusual care as she carried a tray out to the terrace. Not for anything would she mention the meeting. If they could all manage to keep away from the subject perhaps they could have a little while together without Mrs. Manning's forceful personality intruding itself in the family circle.

Mrs. Coleman seated herself on the edge of one of the big green terrace chairs. She always sat up so straight and pert that she didn't need much chair to sit on. Nick's method of occupying a chair was quite different. He liked to sit on the back of his neck and get his feet up on something higher than his head. Mrs. Coleman made a soft *tsk-tsk*ing sound with her tongue which Val knew meant, "Oh, dear! company and no tie!" but Nick merely beamed at her affectionately and she turned to ask Steve about his trip and about whether his mother had left for Germany.

After that she kept the conversational ball skillfully in the air, but Val suspected that she was patting it with only one hand and giving the rest of her attention to disturbing thoughts that were stirring up inside.

From where Mrs. Coleman sat, she could look downhill toward the railroad tracks and the poorer section of town. The sloping, grassy hillside, studded with woods, made the view pleasant enough in the daylight, but now Mrs. Coleman was seeing something through the darkness that was invisible to any but an inner eye. She pulled her chair unhappily about on the terrace.

"I don't like to look downhill any more," she said. "The view is spoiled for me."

"You can't see much of it in the dark," Nick pointed out. "Did something go wrong at your meeting?"

Mrs. Coleman's hands made a despairing little gesture. "Everything went wrong. Mrs. Manning was furious. She left the meeting and of course all of the Seniors left with her."

"Just like a flock of sheep," Nick said cheerfully. "Maybe it's a good thing the Juniors can think for themselves."

"Oh, Nick, how can you!" Mrs. Coleman wailed. "The Juniors are so selfishly concerned with their own little corners that we can't get them to care about the welfare of the town."

Nick nodded. " 'Mrs. Manning says'? Probably they're busy with their babies and their husbands the way they ought to be."

Mrs. Coleman sat up even straighter and her brown eyes fairly snapped. Behind her back Val tried to catch Nick's eye and wig-wag him to stop teasing her.

"That," said her mother, "is a completely shortsighted view. The good of Willow Hill means a lot to every one of us individually. And that means the Juniors, too. But they're afraid to do anything constructive."

Nick looked at Steve. "You got into the game late. We'd better give you a picture of the first quarter. I don't know if you noticed when you were coming up, but the government has put in a new housing project at the foot of the hill. It's to take care of families of men who'll be holding jobs at the Hubbard Plant. This Manning female, who runs all the hen sessions in town, has decided that these people are what she calls undesirable."

"Nick, that's not fair!" Mrs. Coleman cried. "It's not just Mrs. Manning who feels that way. The Juniors don't want them here either, but they won't do anything. We will."

Steve looked a little bewildered. "But I should think any people who moved into as nice a little town as Willow Hill would want to be good citizens."

Mrs. Coleman shook her head. "You don't understand. You see, Stephen, these are Negroes and there is sure to be an undesirable element moving in. We have to do something about it."

Val searched her mind for reassuring words which might furnish oil for badly troubled waters.

"Maybe it won't be so bad," she said. "After all, we have a few Negroes in town and they are all right. We even have a Negro girl in our senior class at school. Her name's Mary Evans and she's a nice, quiet sort of girl. And smart, too. She wrote some good pieces in journalism last semester. They were published in the *Wand.*"

"There are always exceptions, of course," Mrs. Coleman agreed gently, but Val could tell that she hadn't swerved an inch from the course Mrs. Manning had chosen to follow.

At least that seemed to end the discussion for the time being. Silence settled over the terrace. Steve busied himself with the oversized piece of cake Val had cut for him, and Mrs. Coleman stirred her coffee absently, lost in her own distracting thoughts.

Val found herself wishing that the entire subject of the project could be dropped for good. Mrs. Manning was just stirring up trouble. What difference did it make if Negro families *did* occupy those houses at the foot of the hill? They were a long way off and it seemed silly to worry about them. Nobody worried about the ramshackle Negro section over across town. At least these were good new houses, not shacks.

Anyway, the whole subject was beginning to make her feel unpleasantly squirmy inside. It wasn't that she cared so much one way or the other—it was just that she hated unpleasantness.

She yawned a bit elaborately. "I'm getting sleepy and I'll bet Steve's out on his feet. There are some heavy tennis doubles coming up tomorrow and I want my beauty sleep."

A lopsided moon had risen above the hill. Upstairs in her

own room Val could look out her window and watch its radiance etch the town. When she was ready for bed she knelt on the window seat and looked down through the darkness at the gleam of railroad tracks where moonlight touched them. After a while, as her eyes became used to the pattern, she could make out the faint shapes of roofs down there in the project. The sight fascinated her, even though she wanted to turn away from it.

Her mother was always quoting Mrs. Manning on the subject of "rights." What about the rights of those people who'd be moving into the houses?

Oh, well, it wasn't her problem. And there were more pleasant things to think about. There was tomorrow. Tony Millard was coming over tomorrow. True, he was coming to see Judy Piper, but Val Coleman would get to talk to him too. She'd be able to be right in Tony Millard's crowd for a little while.

She wished Steve had turned out to be more attractive. Though, come to think of it, he did have an interesting sort of look. And he was awfully nice. But of course he didn't have what it took to stand up beside somebody like Tony Millard.

Tomorrow she must get up early and see if she could do something about her hair. After all, Judy Piper wouldn't want to be ashamed of her best friend.

CHAPTER 3

DOUBLES

This was Labor Day. The last day of vacation. Val stood before her mirror and untied the blue scarf from about her head for the third time. Judy, in green shorts that set off to advantage her sturdy brown legs, sprawled on Val's bed, tilting her freckled nose at a critical angle.

"That's it, Val! Tie it quick before you lose the effect. It looks super that way."

Val examined her reflection in the mirror. The scarf ends looked rather dashing hanging over her shoulder, and at least the band about her head kept the limp hair out of her face.

She stood back from the mirror trying to get a full length view of herself in white shorts and T-shirt.

Judy patted her tennis racket impatiently against the candlewick spread on Val's bed. "Let's go down and warm up before Tony gets here. You look fine, so stop worrying."

Val frowned at the reflection of a girl who seemed to be all long brown legs and arms. Maybe shorts hadn't been such a good idea. Judy looked all right in shorts, but Val was too tall. Anyway, it was too late to do anything about it now.

Judy bounced off the bed and headed for the stairs. "I brought Dad's racket over for Steve. Dad'll have a fit when he finds out."

"The filial spirit!" Val laughed. "You might try asking your father's permission sometime. Just by way of a novel experiment."

"Goodness no!" Judy caught up the extra racket as they went out the door. "It doesn't do to go encouraging parents at this late date. They're likely to get ideas you'd have to live up to."

Val giggled. For all Judy's sham impudence, there wasn't a happier family in Willow Hill than the Pipers. They argued noisily, borrowed each other's possessions without asking and complained loudly when anyone borrowed theirs. They got into what sounded like the most blood-thirsty squabbles, but everything always ended with love and kisses and comradeship. And they had fun.

Judy's father owned a business in Chicago and the Pipers had larger grounds and a bigger house than the Colemans, who had to get along on the not too impressive salary of a gym teacher. The Pipers belonged to the Country Club and Judy did not always understand the skimping that was necessary to the Coleman family.

The tennis court was at the rear of the Piper house, right at the top of the hill. A high wire fence kept stray balls from bouncing clear to the Willow Hill railroad station.

Beyond the fence, just before the hill dropped steeply away, was a crumbling stone wall. Eight-year-old Debby Piper was an expert at climbing anything which could be climbed and five-year-old Binx was always ready to follow to the best of his ability. The two sat on the wall now, swinging chubby legs and munching apples. Debby was a saucy, miniature Judy, even to her red curls, while Binx was a fair-haired cherub with a talent for getting into trouble. At the moment he was hugging an old basketball in the circle of one fat arm—a ball which had been donated to the cause of youthful activity by Nick Coleman.

Judy waved a threatening racket in their direction. "Remember now. You can chase balls, but you're to stay off the court. If you don't, we'll chase *you*. And don't go bouncing that basketball under our feet."

The two exchanged benign looks and nodded at Judy. You could almost see the wings sprouting. Val got out the balls and the two girls started a lazy volleying back and forth. Stephen Reid must have heard the spat of ball against racket, because he came around from behind the Colemans' to drop into the grass along the edge of the court and watch.

Val felt uneasy and edgy. It was silly for her to worry about Tony's arrival, when it was Judy he was coming to see. But it was past the hour Tony had set and Val couldn't help wondering if he'd changed his mind.

"Hey, wake up!" Judy called, apparently undisturbed by Tony's lateness. "Binx could have got that shot. I thought you'd been getting in some tennis this summer. There's Dad's racket, Steve. You might as well get in on this. Val doesn't seem to be among those present."

And then a car turned into the Piper driveway. No rattletrap, but a low smooth maroon-colored job with the top down. Judy waved her racket.

"Hi, Tony! Come on over."

In spite of herself Val's heart did a queer thump against her ribs. It had better behave—that heart—if it didn't want to go asking for hurts. This was Judy's affair, not Val's. A cute little number like Judy Piper might interest Tony, but never a girl whose main claim to fame was the winning of an essay contest.

He got out of the car and came toward them, cheerful and unhurried. Tony Millard was the sort of boy you liked on sight. He was tall and broad and plenty good-looking, but one of the most winning things about him was the fact that he didn't seem to be aware of his own good looks. If his hair waved a bit in a way the girls liked, that feature was merely a source of irritation to him. He was a regular guy, which accounted for his popularity among the boys as well as the girls.

He threw Val a friendly, "Hi!" that made her feel he was glad to see her there, and acknowledged the introduction to Steve. Then he pulled the case off his racket, took the balls Debby held out and vaulted the net to Judy's side.

Judy said, "We'll toss for partners," and twirled her racket into the air.

Tony caught it over her head. "Nothing doing. We're playing together. Think I'm going to risk having you on the opposite side?"

"The risk is having me on the same side," Judy said cheerfully. "Val's the player—not me."

Val wished she hadn't said that. She had a premonition that she wasn't going to play very well today. The feeling turned out to be right. Steve won the serve and the game was on. It went badly from the beginning. Something was wrong with every shot Val tried. Her racket felt heavy in her hand and she knew Tony had set her down as a dud from her first stroke. Once, in chasing a ball, she collided with Binx, whose job was chasing balls. He was good-natured and didn't mind sitting down hard on the seat of his sun suit pants, but her own awkwardness distressed Val all the more.

"If you're going to give the games away, why don't you let Debby take your racket?" Judy taunted, and Val wanted to shake her. Many were the thumping defeats she'd handed Judy, but now, of all the times she'd have liked to play well—

Anyway, Steve was nice. He caught some of the shots she should have taken and gave her no reproachful looks when she fumbled. Not until Steve's second serve did they win a game. Then, when the score was 4-1, Val looked back toward the house and saw her father standing on the terrace watching.

Grimly she pulled herself together. Nick's eyes upon her made a difference. He had taught her to play tennis and he knew she *could* play. If she let him down as a teacher, she'd hear about it later. Somehow after that she forgot about her legs and the way her hair had slipped out from under the band. A chalky ball left its mark on her hand and she wiped white across her forehead without caring. She was in this now to redeem herself in her father's eyes, and never mind what Tony Millard or anybody else thought about her playing.

Judy was a fair player, but Val knew her weakness. She'd never hurry. Play them fast and drop them right and Judy was helpless. Steve was unexpectedly good and Tony was a whizz. But now the contest lay mostly between Judy and Val and the games were running up on Val's side. When she won the set point with a particularly difficult shot, she knew that she had Tony's respectful attention.

"Wow!" Judy said expressively. "When you get going, Val, there's nobody can touch you. I'm limp. Let's go sit on the wall and rest."

Val glanced toward the terrace and Nick waved his hand. She felt better now. Much better. She hadn't let him down. And evidently the result counted with Tony.

"You're okay," he said as they left the court. "I'd like to take you on in singles sometime."

The warm color in Val's cheeks wasn't due entirely to the heat of the game. She felt as if someone had handed her an orchid.

The others went ahead and Tony talked to her all the way to the wall. "Say—who is this Steve Reid anyway? He's pretty fast on his feet."

She told him about Douglas and Margaret Reid, but he didn't seem too interested in Steve's literary family.

"I was wondering about him for basketball," Tony said. "But if he goes for all that book stuff he probably won't try for the team."

"Why don't you ask him?" Val suggested, feeling suddenly embarrassed by her own bookish achievements.

When they lined up on the wall, she found that Tony had the place between her and Judy, with Steve on her other side. They sat in a row with their backs to the court, looking down through the pleasant woodsy pattern of trees and grass and hillside. Behind them Binx and Debby rested from their labor of chasing tennis balls by bouncing the basketball back and forth between them.

Val wiped some of the chalk from her face and tried vainly to get the blue scarf tied at its original dashing angle. The sun had gone behind a gray cloud bank and it was beginning to look like rain. She hoped it would rain soon so she wouldn't have to play another set of tennis as seriously as the last.

"Tomorrow, school," Tony sounded dejected. "I wish the term was over."

"Why?" Judy asked. "This year should be fun. Being seniors and all that. Don't you like being class president? I should think you'd look forward to it the way Val's looking forward to being editor of the *Wand*."

Val wriggled in embarrassment. "Don't be in such a hurry, Judy. Tony was elected at the close of last semester. But I haven't been appointed yet. For all I know Mary Evans or Sue Peters may get it."

Tony was uninterested in the *Wand*. "That stuff's all right," he said. "And of course there'll be basketball. But Dad says things are going to be bad this year."

"Why bad?" Judy demanded. "Why any more than before?"

Tony nodded toward the houses at the foot of the hill. "That set-up down there. Those shacks going up."

"They're not shacks," Judy said. "They look like pretty nice little houses to me."

"But we don't want those people overrunning the town," Tony protested.

"They have to go somewhere," Judy said reasonably. "Last term Miss Kay was telling us about the crowded conditions on Chicago's south side where most of the Negroes live."

Tony shrugged. "Why don't they go back to Africa where they came from? Dad says that's where they belong."

Val wanted to put her hands over her ears. She was beginning to dislike every mention of the housing project. Just to talk about it made her squirmy again. Was all Willow Hill going to get stirred up about this? As far as she was concerned, she'd like to close her eyes and shut her ears and never see or hear or think about it again. Enough was enough.

But there were the houses at the foot of the hill, a bit stark and bare, standing up against dusty earth with no softening green of trees or shrubbery to give them a—what was the word she wanted? A more *welcoming* look. Well, there would be very little welcome in Willow Hill for the people who were going to move into those houses.

Judy was no respector of opinions she didn't hold with— not even if they belonged to Tony Millard.

She held her hand up, counting on her fingers. "Let's see —there's Scotch in you, Tony, and Irish. And there's a bit of German and French and goodness knows what else."

"I plead guilty," Tony said. "So what?"

"So why don't you go back to Scotland-Ireland-Germany-France where *you* came from, Tony Millard?"

Tony laughed good-naturedly. "That's one up for you, Judy. But I guess maybe it isn't the same thing. Anyway, I don't think they'll be down there long. Not when my Dad and Mrs. Manning get going on this. You can't sit around and watch your own town ruined just because the United States Government is shortsighted enough to dump something like this in your laps."

"Oh, let's not talk about it!" Val cried impatiently. "I'm sick of the whole subject."

Steve had been quiet till now, but she saw that he was looking at her curiously. "What does your father think about it, Val?"

She tried to recall, but somehow she couldn't. He'd teased her mother about Mrs. Manning and her hen sessions, but she couldn't remember his actually stating an opinion one way or the other.

"I don't know," she said. "I guess I've never asked him. Why?"

"Nothing," Steve said. "I was just wondering."

His quiet words made Nick's feeling on the matter seem suddenly important to her. She'd find out about it the first chance she got, she decided.

Judy hopped down from the wall on the side of the sloping hill. "Why don't we find out what we're talking about?" she asked. "Why don't we go down and have a look at those houses? It's too close to lunch time for another game now."

Tony agreed readily enough. "Good idea. Then we can get a sort of before-and-after slant. Dad says the place won't look the same three months from now."

CHAPTER 4

THE PROJECT

The hill was steep and the grass slippery, but this was the quickest way down and who cared about dull matters like sidewalks and roads? Binx and Debby were enthusiastic about any plan for action, and after one half-hearted attempt to make them stay behind, Judy gave up her objections.

Debby could fend for herself, but Binx had adopted Stephen as his special escort and the two of them were making a reasonably cautious descent in the rear. Debby had taken charge of the basketball, ignoring Judy's instructions to leave it behind. When they were nearly down the hill, with Debby well to the fore, the ball slipped out of her hands and went bouncing down the remainder of the steep slope.

Before she had time to go after it, a tall lanky Negro boy stepped out from the shade cast by one of the buildings and caught the ball in one big, long-fingered hand that held it securely while he looked up at the little group on the hillside.

Steve waved and the boy threw the ball. An easy looking overhead toss that covered the distance and dropped into the basket of Steve's waiting hands. The boy gave them all a big smile and disappeared behind a building.

Val was not Nick's daughter for nothing. She knew basketball. "Did you see that?" she cried. "That boy's handled a ball before!"

Even Tony had been impressed by the throw, but it was difficult to accept such skill in a Negro. "Probably a fluke," he said.

"Then it's sure the sort of fluke I'd like to have working for my side on a team," Steve said.

Tony threw him a look of interest. "You going out for basketball?" he asked, and by the time they reached the foot of the hill Tony and Steve were deep in basketball talk. Val felt oddly proud and pleased. She hadn't wanted Tony to condemn Steve for his interest in books and she was glad they were clicking when it came to basketball. Willow High took its basketball seriously. The school had no football team, due to a ruling of the town fathers after a serious accident a few years before. Consequently the whole school threw itself fervently into basketball. Practice started as soon as school opened, and they usually managed to get some neighboring schools to play their team before other communities were thinking much about basketball.

The buildings which made up the project were one-story brick structures, all alike. There were long rows of houses on every block, running together as single units. Each section looked out on space and sunshine front and rear, and there was plenty of room for grass and shrubbery, once they were planted. And the dust wouldn't be so bad when the streets were paved.

"Look," Judy called, "here's a house open for inspection. Maybe we can go in. Do you want to come with us, Debby?

If you don't, you stay right here and watch Binx. You know what mother said."

Debby had seen houses before so she settled for staying outside. She and Binx began a furious tossing of the basket-ball that would have them covered with dust in no time at all.

"Oh well," Judy commented philosophically, "they'll wash."

A Negro woman had come to the door of the display house. She smiled a bit guardedly when she saw the youth of her visitors.

"You may go through if you like," she said. "But please don't touch anything."

Tony mumbled, "What does she think we are?" but Judy shushed him into silence.

"I don't blame her," she whispered. "The way our tribe goes around scribbling down their names and telephone numbers for posterity!"

It was a nice little house, well ordered, bright with new paint and clean varnish. The living room was small, but pleasant. There were two bedrooms, a tiny bathroom with a linoleum floor and shining fixtures. The kitchen had a big window, with a sink beneath it and a modern gas stove. There was even a dining nook with built-in seats, and every-where there was the clean smell of fresh paint.

"It's a honey!" Judy cried, darting about and poking into corners as if she'd been no older than Debby. "Can't you see how it will look when there are plants on the window sills and bright curtains, and pictures on the walls?"

Like Debby, Tony's main interest in life did not lie in

houses. He looked a little bored. "If it just stays like this," he said.

Steve was the surprising one. He examined everything with the interest of a prospective buyer. He tried the window locks and inspected the water faucets and poked into shelf space. If she hadn't been a little on edge, Val would have thought him funny. Somehow she felt uneasy down here and wished they could hurry through their inspection of the house and get back to the pleasant friendliness of the hill. Before something happened.

That was silly. What could possibly happen? She was just getting jumpy about the project because of the way it was being shoved at her on all sides. Beyond the uncurtained kitchen window the clouds were darkening. That made a good excuse.

"Do come along," she said. "It's going to rain."

As she started toward the elbow of hallway that led to the front of the house, she heard voices. She walked around the corner and saw the same tall boy who had tossed the basketball so expertly standing in the tiny corridor. There was a pretty, dark-skinned girl with him whom Val recognized as Mary Evans, the Negro girl in her class in school. In the boy's eyes was the look of someone who had just opened a Christmas package.

"Look at this, Mary!" he cried. "If you move down here so I can come and live with you and Dad, I won't have to share a bathtub with six other families."

This was a private conversation she had happened upon and Val stood still in embarrassment, wondering whether to retreat or to make her presence known. At that moment the girl looked her way. A moment before she had seemed friendly and prettier than Val had realized, but when she saw Val an unhappy change came over her. The light died out of her smoky dark eyes, the smile left her lips and something careful and guarded and vaguely hostile came into her manner.

"Hello, Mary," Val said quickly. "We came down to look at the project. The houses are really nice. Are you going to move into one?"

The boy was smiling his big friendly grin again, but there was no warmth in Mary's voice when she answered, though she spoke quietly enough.

"We've put in our application for a house and we're hoping to be accepted. This is my brother, Jeff."

"Hello, Jeff," Val said, feeling somehow ill-at-ease.

The group in the kitchen, hearing voices, had followed Val and they all went into the living room where there was space enough to spread out. Val introduced Jeff a little awkwardly and then rushed into words.

"I didn't know you had a brother, Mary." She turned to Jeff. "Will you be coming to Willow High?"

Come to think of it, she didn't know much about Mary at all, though she'd known her all through high school. The girl had always been a quiet shadow who wore neat dark clothes and was soft-spoken and well-mannered. Probably the only time she had ever seemed like a real person to Val was when she had written those pieces that had been published in the *Wand*.

But now the contrast she had glimpsed of an eager, excited, hopeful girl, supplanted so quickly by one who was cold and guarded, was startling. Here was someone very real whom she had never seen before.

Mary answered for her brother in the same quiet tone, from which all emotion had been suppressed. "Jeff has been living in Chicago with an aunt. He'll be a junior at school."

"I hope you'll go in for basketball, Jeff," Steve said. "That was some throw you made a little while ago."

The boy was openly delighted. "I'd sure like to get on the team if there's a place for me," he said.

Tony had gone to look out a window and Val sensed disapproval in the set of his shoulders. "It's going to rain all right," he said abruptly. "We'd better get along." He went past the others to the door without waiting.

"See you in school tomorrow, Mary," Judy said. "So long, Jeff. I'd better go collect my young-uns."

Except for Tony's abruptness, their exit was reasonably casual. Outside Debby was drawing dragons in the dust with a stick and Binx was nowhere in sight.

"Oh Debby!" Judy wailed. "Where is he? I told you to watch!"

Debby looked around in amazement at a horizon empty of Binx. "But he was right here, Judy. He was playing with the ball. Honest, he was."

"A lot of good if he isn't here now," Judy scolded. "Come on, kids, spread out. We've got to find Binx before that storm breaks."

It wasn't difficult to find him. The searching party scattered to the rear of the row of nearest buildings and there was Binx, happily pulling a red wagon in which sat a beaming little Negro boy clutching the basketball against his stomach. Over against a wall stood a small Negro girl of about Debby's age—a leggy little thing, watching the other two with lively interest.

Binx waved happily. "I gotta friend!" he chortled. "His name's Peanuts."

"Tell your friend goodby," Judy commanded. "It's going to rain and we have to get home fast."

Debby ran over to help Binx with the wagon, but before she reached him a small dark whirlwind flew into action. The leggy child by the wall flung herself across the intervening space and pushed Debby from behind as hard as she could push. Debby, taken completely by surprise, sprawled in the dust. She got up with skinned knees and tears of rage in her eyes. Before the Negro girl could fly to safety, Debby had slapped her hard across one cheek, and if Judy and Val hadn't collared the two and pulled them apart, more blood would have been shed.

The sound of the fray brought Mary running out of the house to put soothing arms around the Negro child, while Judy quieted Debby.

"We're awfully sorry," Judy told Mary. "I don't understand quite what happened."

"We are *not* sorry!" Debby cried. "I wasn't doing nothing to her and she pushed me. She—she just *pushed* me!"

"*Anything* to her," Judy corrected absently. "And you shouldn't have slapped. No matter what—you shouldn't have slapped."

Mary Evans, however, seemed not too interested in explanations of what had happened. She led her weeping charge back into the house with scarcely a glance at the others.

"What a mess!" Judy said, wiping futilely at Debby's scraped knees. But Val knew she didn't mean just the knees. The whole affair had been sudden and ugly and apparently

without reason. They started back uphill in a silence broken
only by Debby's sniffles.

"I certainly don't see why she did that," Val said. "There
was no sense to it at all."

Tony agreed, "It's just like dad says—you can't go mixing
races and expect to get along. I don't think it's a good idea
to get that kid's hopes up about being on the team."

Tony had been captain of the basketball team last year
and probably would be again this year, Val thought. If he
were against having Jeff play—

In spite of what had happened to Debby, Judy was trying
to be fair. "Oh, I don't know. Maybe the team could do with
a player like Jeff Evans."

After that everyone seemed to be too much out of breath
from climbing to talk. The rain broke just as they reached
the top of the hill and they scattered for shelter. Judy invited Tony to come over to the Pipers' till it stopped, but he
made a dive for his car and Steve went over to help him get
the top up.

Val went upstairs to her room to get cleaned up for lunch,
feeling that what had started out to be a wonderful day had
somehow gone thoroughly awry. Her mother's voice summoned her and she gave herself a last hopeless look in the
mirror before she went downstairs.

"Where did you young people disappear to this morning?"
Mrs. Coleman asked when they were all settled at the table.

Val looked at her plate. "Judy thought we ought to go
down and see the project houses."

"Whatever for?" There was surprise in her mother's tone.

"Oh—just curiosity, I guess." Val tried to shrug the matter
off.

"We ran into a fellow who could throw a basketball better than I've ever seen one thrown," Steve said. "With one hand, too."

"What was he doing down there?" Mrs. Coleman asked.

Val hurried to explain. "It was Mary Evans' brother. They're going to live in one of those houses."

"Anyway he sure looks like material for the team," Steve persisted. Apparently he was almost as sold on basketball as Tony.

Mrs. Coleman glanced up from passing a basket of rolls and there was concern in her eyes. "Perhaps you don't understand the situation, Stephen. If he's a Negro boy I'm sure Nick won't want him on the team."

Nick concentrated on stirring his coffee while they all looked at him. "I guess I'll put anybody on the team who can play basketball," he said.

"Butter, Stephen?" Mrs. Coleman asked. "And that guava jelly's especially good. But, Nick, there never has been a Negro boy on a Willow High team. Don't you think it would make it difficult in lots of ways?"

"Oh, I don't know." Nick sipped his coffee and helped himself to more sugar.

Val remembered what Stephen Reid had asked that morning about what Nick thought of all this. She hadn't been able to tell him then.

She leaned toward her father. "Nick, what about all this? What about Negroes coming to Willow Hill and to high school? I mean what do you think about it?"

He smiled at her. "I think America gets a bit mixed up sometimes. Maybe this will be a good chance for some of us to get our thinking straight and find out a couple of things.

Seems to me people are people. If a kid plays good basketball, I want him on the team and I don't much care if he's
pink or green or polka dotted. And I guess I don't give a
hang what anybody else thinks of his color either."

"Oh, dear," Mrs. Coleman said unhappily. But for once
she was without a handy quotation from Mrs. Manning.

"What do you think, Val?" her father asked.

She didn't know how to answer that. Probably she was
just one of the mixed-up ones. Until lately she hadn't
thought much about the subject at all. Miss Kay had talked
about it some last year in school, but it had been something
to be vaguely sorry about—like people starving in India, or
dying in a flood in China. It hadn't anything to do with *her*.

Now it was beginning to concern her. It meant something
her mother was getting excited about. It meant looking at a
Mary Evans she had never seen before and wondering what
went on behind that quiet mask she wore.

It meant feeling a strong sense of injustice when that little
Negro girl had rushed so unfairly upon Debby. It meant
feeling that her father and Steve were right, and if Jeff
Evans played good basketball he *ought* to be on the team.
And it meant liking Tony Millard awfully well and wanting
to sympathize with what he thought.

In fact, it meant mostly—confusion. She shook her head at
Nick. "I guess I don't know what I think," she said. "So how
about changing the subject?"

CHAPTER 5

EDITORIAL APPOINTMENT

The first day of school was always exciting. Greeting people you hadn't seen all summer, exclaiming over new hair-do's, trying to have snappy come-backs ready when the boys teased you. Not being able to speak two consecutive sensible words to anybody, because someone else would always dash up to interrupt.

More people knew about her essay than she'd expected, Val discovered, and Judy of course was helping the publicity along. She and Judy managed to get lockers together and she noted that Tony had annexed the one beside Judy's.

But she mustn't stand here in the corridor chattering. In the excitement she had almost forgotten about Stephen Reid. She knew Miss Kay would want to meet him, so she rescued Steve from Judy who had him cornered while she raved about her favorite club project.

"I suppose it will seem queer graduating from a new school," Val commented as she led the way through the noisy corridor to the principal's office.

"Not so strange," Steve said. "Dad and mother were always moving around, so I haven't any roots. If mother and I weren't following Dad on some assignment to Washington or San Francisco or New York, Dad and I would be following

mother to New England or some other place because she
wanted to write a novel about California."

Val blinked. "New England to write about California?"

Steve grinned. "You don't know novelists. When they
want to write about Brazil they go to Canada and vice-versa.
It's called getting perspective."

The racket in the corridor was deafening and they gave
up trying to talk. It was always like this the first few days.
Then you got used to the slamming of locker doors and the
echo of voices down the hallways and you scarcely noticed
the noise at all. Inside the office it was a little quieter and
while they waited to see the principal Val explained about
her to Steve.

"Miss Kay is what makes Willow High click. You'll like
her. You never saw so much pep. She'd make a good cheer-
leader. She teaches journalism, too, so if you take that you'll
be in her class. And of course she's the teacher-adviser on
the *Wand* and heads the committee that appoints the editor."

A few minutes later they wriggled through the crowd of
girls in sloppy Joes and plaid skirts and boys in slacks and
open-collared shirts to the door of Miss Kay's private office.

The principal looked up as they stood in the doorway.
"Hello, Val. Come in. Congratulations on your article."

Val flushed with pleasure as she drew Steve into the room.
"This is Stephen Reid, Miss Kay. He's staying at our house
while his mother is in Europe. Maybe you know the things
his mother and father have written—Douglas and Margaret
Reid."

Miss Kay held out her hand. "We're glad to have you
here, Stephen," she said.

That was all. No flowery stuff about his parents. Just a sincere indication that she was ready to like and respect him for whatever he was in his own right. Miss Kay was like that.

Val backed toward the door. "I'll take Steve over to get properly enrolled now. I wanted you to meet him first."

As Steve went into the corridor the principal stopped Val. "I *am* proud of you. But if you'd work as hard in journalism as you must have done on that piece, I'd be even prouder."

Val felt somewhat let down as she joined Steve. If Miss Kay was right—well, she didn't want to think about it just then.

In the corridor they passed Jeff and Mary Evans and Val spoke to them. Jeff said hello with his usual big grin, but Mary went by as if she had not heard.

Val pitched her voice indignantly against the uproar. "What's the matter with her? Do you suppose she's mad because Debby slapped that little girl yesterday? Why didn't she stay around long enough to get the story straight? The child deserved a good spanking."

"Maybe she thinks we're angry at her," Steve said.

"Oh, well," Val shrugged the subject aside. "Isn't Miss Kay nice?"

"Swell," Steve agreed. "She made me feel I could fit in right away. Look—suppose you go on back to your gang. I can take care of myself from here in."

She was a little relieved to get away. First day back in school was exciting and she didn't want to miss all the fun. Besides, there was the possibility of the *Wand* editor appointment coming up today and that made it difficult to concentrate on anything else.

As she hurried back along the crowded corridor and up-

stairs to her division room, she thought how small the freshmen looked this year, how terribly young. Each new crop
seemed younger than those of the year before. Or was it that
the seniors were a little older and had forgotten how young
and small they had once been?

Judy waited for her impatiently in the upstairs hall. "What
happened to you? Tony's holding down seats so we can all be
together. Come along!"

It was nice to be included in Tony Millard's plans. As she
dropped into the seat he'd been holding practically by football tactics, he said, "Don't forget—tennis singles first chance
we get."

She was pleased, but a little uneasy. After all, Judy had
first claim and she didn't want to cut in.

"When will Kay come across with the *Wand* appointment?" Judy turned around in the seat ahead of Val.

"Sh-sh!" Val whispered. "Think how silly I'll look if you
go shouting around about me being editor and then I don't
get it."

But there wasn't much uncertainty in her. Miss Kay knew
about her essay, had even read it. Of course she had made
that remark about her not working very hard in journalism,
but surely Miss Kay knew how hard she would work if she
landed the coveted editorship.

She glanced at Tony. Maybe if she got to be editor she
might seem just a little more important in his eyes. Even if
putting words on paper wasn't a talent that would much im-
press him, holding an important school offce might be.

"You didn't answer my question," Judy persisted.

"Oh—that. She usually does it in journalism the first day.
That is, after she's conferred with the committee so that

they're all in agreement. That's probably been arranged during the summer."

When Steve came in he found an empty seat across the room. Val noted that Mary Evans had taken an unobtrusive place at the rear. She sat with a pencil in her hand, drawing lean-limbed fashion model ladies all over a piece of paper, paying no attention to noisy conversation on every side.

Val noted with a faint sense of surprise that she was wearing an unusually good-looking dress. It was dark and plain, with white at the throat, but it had the design and cut of an expensive dress. Funny, she had never really looked at Mary in a way that saw anything until yesterday. Now, for the first time, she felt a little curious about her as a person.

The bell rang shrilly and chatter died down. It was odd how you jumped at the bell the first day and then got so used to it again it didn't startle you at all. Mrs. Harcourt was their division teacher this year. She had a rep for being heavy on discipline, but other senior classes had survived her reign, so this one probably would too.

The usual routine of getting schedules drawn up began and the seniors applied themselves to juggling periods. Val looked quickly to see when journalism came. Last period. How could she ever live that long? She wouldn't be able to draw a really comfortable breath until that matter was settled. But she mustn't worry. It was true that there were others in the class who had done some fair writing—Mary Evans was one. But Val suddenly felt that in the final showdown she could write circles around anyone else in school.

There were ideas she had for the *Wand*. She wanted her editorship to go down as being one of the best the school had ever known. She wanted to work in a better system of news coverage, for one thing. Sometimes the stuff published was pretty awful. Too kiddish. Too corny. And there should be more editorial pieces like the one which had won the contest for her. Perhaps she could do some others along that line.

It might be a good idea to read her printed piece over again to see if it would give her a lead on some similar ideas. Come to think of it, she hadn't read that piece for more than a week. When it had first been published, she'd read it a dozen times a day regularly until she'd worn out her first clipping and had had to start on another one.

It had been thrilling to read her own words in print. They had seemed so much better than they'd ever been in the original manuscript. But after a while even she had got a little tired of reading those remarkable words. Tonight, however, she'd get it out again and read it with new purpose as editor of the *Wand*.

The day droned on lazily, hot and clear and blue. It was still bright summer. No hint of September haze in the air. Not a cloud in the sky. The patch of it that could be seen all day long beyond Willow High's windows was still clear blue by the time last period rolled around and Val felt excited anticipation over the approaching journalism class.

Tony didn't go in for literary subjects so he would not be present to enjoy her little triumph, but undoubtedly Judy would build it up to him in her usual enthusiastic manner. Judy was always generous about giving everyone due credit.

When they had taken their places in the journalism room, Miss Kay gave Val a little flutter right away by holding up before the whole class the paper which contained her piece.

She wanted them all to read it, she said. Those who hadn't might borrow her copy.

"We're very proud of Val," she concluded. "Not just because she has achieved publication at her age. We realize that this is a special occurrence and not to be expected in the normal course of events. I don't want to detract from Val's glory, but it is wise to recognize that this award doesn't mean that she has reached the status of a successful writer, but only that in competing with other young people her age, she has produced something outstanding.

"If she will remember that it may save her later disappointments that are sure to come. Now if our young celebrity will apply herself equally well this coming term, perhaps we can expect even better things of her."

Oh, she would! Val promised herself fervently. She'd never be guilty of slipshod work again just because writing came so easily to her. Only let her land the editorship of the *Wand* and she'd work harder than she'd ever worked before in her life.

But Miss Kay delayed the anxiously awaited appointment till the last five minutes before the bell. When the time came she spoke into a pin-drop silence.

"I know you're all wondering about the *Wand* staff," she said. "So perhaps I'd better end the suspense. As you know, I have consulted with a committee of teachers who are familiar with the talents and weaknesses of each one of you and are in agreement with me in their choice of editor."

Val held her breath. Why didn't she hurry and get to the point? All these preliminaries were maddening. The principal glanced her way, but somehow without recognition in her eyes, and Val felt a sudden chill of doubt. But she *had*

to get this! Suddenly she wanted it more than she had ever
wanted anything in her life. And surely everyone expected
her to get it.

There was something disturbingly grave about Miss Kay's
expression, as if she knew that what she was about to an-
nounce might hurt someone.

Her words came quietly to the listening room. "Because
of her merit as a writer, because she has worked so hard and
faithfully for the good of the paper, the committee is ap-
pointing Mary Evans as editor-in-chief of the *Willow
Wand."*

There was a surprised silence and then a smattering of
polite applause, ended quickly by the bell. All around her
people were getting up from their seats. Val rose automati-
cally. It was hard to realize what had happened. She mustn't
let anyone know how she felt—that was the main thing just
now. To pretend she didn't care, that she hadn't expected
the editorship herself.

She felt Judy's hand on her arm, looked down into Judy's
sympathetic eyes. Judy knew. And because Judy knew, Val
pulled quickly away from her. Sympathy right now might
make her cry. As she turned she saw Mary rising from her
own seat at the back of the room.

Nick always said the important thing was not the fact of
losing, but how you took defeat. Whatever happened, you
made the right gestures. You were a good sport.

"Come along," she said to Judy.

They moved toward the back of the room where Mary was
picking up her things. "Congratulations, Mary," Val said. "I
know you'll do a swell job."

There was nothing in Mary's manner to show that this

was a big moment in her life. She said, "Thank you," gravely, and Val thought with a surge of bitterness that the other girl didn't care.

She heard Judy rushing into words beside her, tiding them through an awkward moment. There were a few others congratulating Mary, but they did not look at Val. She stepped back from the little group, anxious to escape, but before she turned away Mary's eyes met hers for a startling instant. Her lips might be still and unsmiling, but Val had a brief glimpse of the exultant triumph in her eyes. Then Mary's long black lashes swept down and the exultance was hidden.

Val walked to the door and into the corridor with her head held high, her lips closed tightly to prevent any wayward quivering. Later she could let down, but not now. She walked along the hall toward her division room and went to her seat. One or two people tried to murmur consoling remarks, but she brushed past them as if she didn't hear.

It was Tony who broke through her defense. Someone had told him and he looked genuinely sorry. But he looked mad, too.

"That was a lousy deal," he said as she slipped into her seat. "You don't have to take it lying down."

Even in her rising misery his words helped a little. It mattered to Tony Millard that she hadn't been chosen as editor. But the danger of tears was even closer now. She bent over her desk and did not look his way again.

CHAPTER 6

"IT'S NOT HOW YOU WIN—"

The room was stilled for dismissal and Val waited numbly. It was better to stay numb until she could be alone. The worst thing of all would be to let Tony know how much this hurt.

She wished she could escape him when the room was dismissed, but he gave her no chance. He came right to her locker when they went out in the corridor, hardly noticing Judy who was at his elbow.

"Why don't you go after Kay on this?" he asked. "Put her on the spot. Tell her you want to know why Mary got it instead of you. The class will back you up."

"Oh, I couldn't!" Val cried. "It doesn't matter anyway. I don't care."

"Sure you do," Tony told her. "A job like that shouldn't go to Mary Evans. A white girl ought to get it. This'll just make trouble in the school."

Judy put her hand on Val's arm. "Don't think I don't sympathize with Val. But maybe this will be good for the school. Maybe with all the new Negro students who'll be coming up here we need to do something like this."

Tony shook his head. "My Dad says—"

But whatever Wayne Millard's opinion of the matter

might be, Val didn't hear it just then. She was rescued from the necessity for listening by a girl who touched her sleeve.

"Miss Kay wants you in her office. Right away, please."

She slammed her locker shut. She had no particular desire to see Miss Kay at this moment, but it was better than standing here listening to Tony's sympathetic indignation.

"I'll be waiting around to see how you come out," he told her.

There was nothing she could say to him. Whatever he expected of her she couldn't do.

Miss Kay was waiting in her office and Mary Evans stood beside her desk.

"Come in, Val." Miss Kay's tone was unusually gentle. "Mary and I have been talking over possible appointments for the rest of the *Wand* staff. We'll certainly need your help."

A lot she cared about any other place if she couldn't be editor, Val thought. What did they think she was? She wanted to walk indignantly out of the room. But she had listened to Nick's voice so many times when he'd harangued the team that she could almost hear it now.

"It's how you lose that matters. If you get beaten in fair play, you take it and grin. Maybe you try to do better next time, but this time. . . ."

This time. Now. Fair play. Never mind the hurt place inside that was beginning to wake up and ache. Hide that. At all costs hide the wounds of the vanquished from the winner's eyes; especially when this winner was so triumphant over her success. Val stood quietly where she was, waiting.

"Mary and I want you to be the associate editor, Val. That's right, isn't it, Mary?"

"Yes, Miss Kay." Mary's tone was soft, agreeable.

Val flashed her a quick look. She didn't believe in that gentle agreement. Val Coleman would be the last person Mary would want on the staff. She'd want to run things her own way, not listen to advice from a might-have-been-editor.

She spoke lightly, flippantly, putting on as good an act as Mary's. "I guess you'd better get someone else. I'm going to be awfully busy this term anyway."

Without waiting for an answer, Val hurried out the door. She half expected Miss Kay to call her back, but the principal let her go in silence.

She felt an immediate reaction of shame for her hasty words, and was relieved to see that the corridor was nearly empty and that Tony Millard was nowhere in sight. Probably he'd forgotten about waiting to hear how things came out. If only she could escape without running into him. Tony was the last person she could bear to face right now.

There was a side entrance that would lead her to a roundabout way home, but she didn't care. She knew exactly where she meant to go and she could last that long, holding all her emotions in check, choking back the hurt.

She almost ran the last block and scurried around the Pipers' past the tennis court to the stone wall. There was a place where the stones were worn smooth from scrambling young feet and just beyond was a secret hollow, where wall and bush and trees crowded in around a little circle of grass to make a hiding place.

For as long as she could remember Val had come here in unhappy moments. She knew she could fling herself down on the grass and bury her head in her arms and there would be no eyes to see, no ears to hear, no well-meaning tongues to instruct and advise.

Tears were already wet on her cheeks before her toe was on the lowest stone. She let them come, pulling herself up to the flat top of the wall, dropping down into the hollow of grass on the other side without stopping to look first—without stopping to see that someone else had discovered her hiding place and was there before her.

Stephen Reid lay stretched on his back on the grass, his hands clasped beneath his head, his eyes upon the distant blue of the sky.

Before he could turn and take a good look she rubbed the back of her hand against her eyes, brushing away the tears. She couldn't go back over the wall. This was nearly the end of her rope. She slipped down into the warm grass and concentrated once more on not crying.

The summer world was quiet. The town sounds of Willow Hill were something in the distance. The sky was blue and cloudless as it had been all day and no breeze stirred.

How quiet Steve was. Why didn't he say something? He hadn't moved a muscle since she'd jumped down from the wall. She stole a quick look at him. Yes he had. He'd closed his eyes. He looked as if he'd gone to sleep and she began to feel unreasonably annoyed. A nice, sympathetic guy he was! A lady with a shattered life dropped over the wall and he went to sleep. She blew her nose crossly.

He didn't open his eyes, but he spoke to her for the first time since she'd dropped down beside him on the grass.

"Go ahead and cry if you want to," he said. "I don't mind."

She felt even more annoyed because she hadn't fooled

him. He knew perfectly well why she'd come here, but apparently he didn't have sense enough to go away.

"I don't care about having an audience," Val said coldly.

"Who's watching you? I'm not even listening."

He was horrible. Men were all like that. Inconsiderate and unsympathetic. Judy would have soothed and patted her and really understood.

"I'm never going to write another word," Val told the world in general. "I'm through for good."

"Well, that will tell the story," Steve said.

She wanted to ignore him, to pretend she hadn't heard.

"Tell what story?" The question came out without her help.

He was looking at her now. "I mean it will show whether or not you're a writer. Lots of people want to be, but they give up when something goes wrong. The others write no matter what."

Steve was different from any boy she'd ever known. He sounded older than the others. Probably because he'd been so much around people like Margaret and Doug, who had treated him as if he was their own age and not just a kid.

But she didn't feel like being a good sport any longer. "It isn't fair," she protested. "I've worked all through high school for this one thing. I've put everything I could into it. My work on that essay—everything."

"Then it certainly isn't fair," Steve agreed.

There, that was a little better. At least he was beginning to see it her way.

"After all," he went on lazily, his eyes closed again, "you're the final judge of how much you deserved it. Nobody knows better than you how hard you tried."

She didn't like the sound of that. "I suppose you think I didn't try! I suppose you don't believe—"

"No. I just said you're the one who knows."

They were silent after that. It was as if he'd set a mirror down in front of her. She hadn't really looked into that mirror till now and she didn't like what she saw there. She wanted to push it away.

"But Mary's going to cause trouble as editor. She'll put things into the *Wand* that will make everybody mad. Steve, you should have seen the look in her eyes when I went to congratulate her. She looked happy in a—a triumphant sort of way. I can't explain it." Val sat up suddenly. "You know what her look reminds me of?"

"What?"

"Of the way that little girl looked who jumped out to push Debby yesterday. That child was glad to push Debby down and Mary was glad I'd been beaten. If I'd won I'd have been happy, but I wouldn't have been glad someone else was unhappy."

"Gosh, I don't know the answers," Steve said. "But I guess we have to remember we've been pushing them down for more than a hundred years. Maybe we'd feel like that too, in their place."

"But if they want us to like them, why—" she paused, "oh, well. I don't know the answers either. And what do you think—Miss Kay asked me to be associate editor of the *Wand!*"

"Good for her," Steve approved.

"You don't suppose I accepted? I don't want second place and I wouldn't work with Mary. I'd be the last person she'd want for an associate anyway. That was Miss Kay's idea."

Steve didn't answer. He picked up a twig and gave an unwelcome boost to an ant that was trying to cross a grass blade bridge. A moment later he got to his feet and stood looking down through the bushes toward the project houses.

"Something's wrong," he said. "There's trouble down there."

His tone brought Val up beside him. She could look downhill toward the houses and see a group of boys scattering through the streets. White boys. Even as she looked she saw an arm raised to throw and a moment later heard the crash of breaking glass.

Steve went straight through the bushes on his plunge downhill, and without weighing or deciding Val went after him.

CHAPTER 7

TROUBLE STARTS

Before they reached the foot of the steep grassy slope, Val saw that a man was ahead of them. All but one of the boys had lit out as fast as their legs could carry them the moment the glass crashed, but the man had collared the boy who'd thrown the stone.

Even as she slipped and stumbled down the hill in her haste, Val recognized her father. When she and Steve came out on the dusty street beside him, Nick had the boy by the scruff of his neck and was shaking him hard.

"What's the idea?" Nick said. "Why did you break that window?"

The boy twisted around in Nick's grasp and Val saw that it was Tony Millard's younger brother, Hank. He was a boy of twelve and big for his age, but Nick's fingers on his collar were so much steel. He looked frightened and defiant at the same time.

"Your dad won't think much of this," Nick said, giving him another shake. "Wayne Millard doesn't hold with property damage."

Hank stopped wriggling and stood still. He looked like a younger edition of Tony, and Val wished it had been anyone but Tony's brother her father had caught.

"Dad doesn't care what I do down here." The youngster was inclined to be cocky, now the shaking had stopped. "Nobody in Willow Hill cares. Everybody wants to get these Negroes outta here."

"*I* care," Nick said sternly. "I don't think much of guys who go around throwing stones through windows."

"Lemme go!" Hank demanded, squirming again.

Nick loosened his grip and the boy wriggled free. But he didn't run now. He stood his ground, facing the school coach insolently.

"Who cares what you think? Everybody knows you're a lousy coach. Can't even turn out a good basketball team!"

He didn't wait for an answer, but ducked out of reach and walked off, swaggering a bit and scuffing up the dust with his feet. Val wanted to run after him and give him a good shaking for her own satisfaction. The nerve of the kid—talking like that to Nick Coleman!

A woman had come out on the steps of the house where the window had been broken, and the attendant in charge was crossing the road from the display house over the way. The first woman looked frightened, the second one angry.

"I'm sorry I couldn't get here in time to stop them," Nick said. "But I know the boy who threw the rock. I think his father will make good on the damage."

The little boy who had played with Binx yesterday was clinging to his mother, crying, not knowing what he was crying about. He was frightened by the noise and the raised voices of grown-ups.

The woman patted his cheek and spoke anxiously to Nick. "Maybe we'd better just mend the window and let it go. We don't want to make trouble. We just want to be let alone."

"I'll report it," the attendant said. "We can't start out by overlooking this sort of thing. Thank you for coming over."

When he'd given the women Wayne Millard's name, Nick looked around at Steve and Val. "Hello, you two. Where did you drop from?"

"I saw what happened, sir," Steve said, "and I came down to see if I could stop those kids. But you got here first."

Now that the incident was over, Val realized how tired her father looked. She wanted again to get her hands on Hank Millard and shake him dizzy. Had that spiteful crack he'd made hurt Nick? Anybody knew it took more than a coach to make a winning team. You had to have good material in the first place, and Willow High had had bad luck on that score for some time. It wasn't Nick's fault that Tony was the only real player on the team.

"I was heading toward town," Nick said. "Guess I'll be on my way. So long, kids. It's too bad this happened."

When he had gone Steve and Val turned back toward the hill.

"More trouble," Val said. "I expect mother and Mrs. Manning and Wayne Millard are right. With that project opening up all we're going to see is trouble. You can't just go changing a whole social system, Steve." How often she'd heard her mother quote Mrs. Manning on that!

"Binx made his own social system yesterday," Steve said, "and it seemed to be working fine."

"Binx is a baby. He doesn't know any better."

"Maybe he won't know any better unless somebody tells him."

Val thought about that a moment. "Debby didn't know any different either—until that little Negro girl pushed her down. I'll bet she started getting a few prejudices right then."

Steve paused in his climb and swung an arm about the trunk of a tree to anchor himself. "I can't help wondering what happened to that child that we don't even know about that made her want to push Debby?"

"Nothing happened to her, probably." Val sat down on a rock that jutted from the hillside. "She was just mean."

"We don't know that. I expect other kids have pushed Debby down and she probably hasn't stayed hurt or mad very long. But because this child *looks* different, Debby's likely to connect the hurt with the color of the child's skin and remember it a lot longer. Of course it works the other way, too. I mean that probably that little Negro girl was remembering some hurt that was connected with white skin, and when she saw an opportunity to hurt someone who looked like those who had hurt her, she just went to it."

"Maybe," Val said, but she wasn't convinced.

Steve looked down toward the houses, quiet now in the sunshine. "Dad used to talk about these things sometimes. He said if enough people in the world believed that everybody with red hair ought to be outcasts and if they pounded that idea into their kids when they were growing up, then that's what we'd all believe."

Val laughed. "And I wouldn't dare be friends with Judy?"

"That's it. Sounds kind of silly, doesn't it?"

"It is silly." Val dismissed the idea flatly. "Red-haired people are just like anybody else."

"Maybe we're all just like anybody else."

Val could think of lots of people she wasn't like at all. But she didn't want to quarrel with Steve. Somehow her earlier annoyance with him seemed to have evaporated. Maybe he wasn't exciting the way Tony Millard was, but you could talk to him about things you could never discuss with Tony. And it was fun to have someone to talk to, even if it was only to disagree.

"You know, Steve," she said, "you sound like your father a lot. I mean you sound the way he used to write."

"I'm glad if I do," he said quietly. "I don't know anybody I'd rather sound like."

"But isn't it sort of—oh, discouraging to have a mother and father like yours?" She was thinking of the way her mother was so pretty and wanted so much to have an attractive daughter.

"Discouraging? Well, maybe it would be if I kept thinking about what they've done and how far ahead of me they are. But when I think about all the things *I* haven't done and want to do—"

"Do you want to write? I notice you're taking journalism at school."

He was looking off into the distance and there was a dream in his eyes. "Maybe it's crazy, but I guess what I'd like some day is to run a newspaper."

"Run a newspaper?"

"Oh, not a big paper. Not even a paper in as big a town as Willow Hill. But maybe a paper in some little country town where they needed a good **one**. Then I suppose I'd write. News and editorials and everything that goes in a paper."

Perhaps that wasn't a very glittering sort of ambition, but somehow Val sympathized with it. She had an idea that he'd make an awfully good small town editor if he really went into it.

Steve unwound himself from about the tree trunk and started uphill again with Val following. When they reached the "secret" hollow and climbed over the wall, she remembered with distaste her aching hurt of less than a half hour before. Not that she had forgotten her disappointment. It was still there at the back of her mind, but the matters which had intervened since had made it seem less important.

The fear in the eyes of that woman whose house had been stoned had been more important than her own disappointment. The thing Hank Millard had said about her father—even if it was untrue—had hurt him and that was important.

"I'm beginning to understand," she said as they reached the terrace behind the house. "I mean what you said about novelists going to New England to get perspective so they could write about California. Maybe we all need to go off and get a taste of another kind of life once in a while so we can see our own more clearly. There! How's that for the Girl Philosopher?"

"I guess that *is* the idea," Steve said, and for some reason she felt better inside.

Mrs. Coleman was at the telephone when they came into the house. She looked more like an older sister than a mother, Val thought with a flash of pride—so trim and neat and young in her blue polka dot dress with the fluffy ruffles that became her so well. She had washed her hair and damp little tendrils still clung to the nape of her neck. But as she set the phone down and turned to greet them, Val saw the mark of worry between her brows. Mrs. Manning again? she wondered.

Her mother confirmed her suspicion. "Val, honey, why didn't you tell me what happened at school today? I mean about losing out on the *Wand*. Dorothy Manning carried the news home and her mother just phoned me. She's really very disturbed."

Val was becoming more and more tired of Mrs. Manning and she never had cared for Dorothy. "Why should she be disturbed?"

Her mother's hands fluttered vaguely. "She thinks something should be done about it."

"What can anybody do about it? If the committee wanted to appoint Mary Evans, it's up to them."

"But, Val, you deserved it! That essay. Everyone feels you deserved it. I don't see how Miss Kay could allow anything so unfair."

"I don't know whether I deserved it or not," Val said, and felt a little surprised at her own words. Before she had talked to Steve she had been perfectly sure. "Anyway, I don't think Mrs. Manning ought to meddle. It's not her business."

"She feels that it is everyone's business. She's trying to get up some sort of meeting."

"About the editorship?" Val asked in dismay.

"Not just that. About this whole matter of the housing project. I—somehow I feel it's going a little far, but she has attended rallies of the same sort in Chicago and she thinks it is the only thing to do."

Val started up the stairs. "Just so they leave me out of it."

"But, honey, this appointment of Mary Evans is just the sort of thing which ought to be avoided at this time. Mrs.

Manning has some influence with the school board and she may be able to bring enough pressure to bear on Miss Kay so that you'll be made editor after all."

Val paused with her hand on the banister. "Mother, *please* don't let them interfere. Of course I felt bad about it at first. I suppose I still do. But I don't want to be editor that way. I really didn't work as hard as Mary did. And they did ask me to be associate editor."

Her mother looked shocked. "Of course you refused?"

"Yes," Val said in a small voice, "I refused." She had a feeling that she could talk for the next three hours about this and her mother would just keep on quoting Mrs. Manning and not really understand at all.

"Perhaps a meeting is the only answer," Mrs. Coleman mused. "If the town will just work as one unit we may be able to force them out before trouble starts."

Steve had been standing quietly at the rear of the hall and now he spoke for the first time. "Trouble has already started, Mrs. Coleman. A gang of seventh and eighth grade boys were breaking windows this afternoon down in the project."

There was fright in Mrs. Coleman's eyes. "There! You see? We have to do something quickly. Mrs. Manning is right."

She turned back to the telephone and Val went upstairs to her own room. She closed the door and sat down on her bed. But she didn't want to think. There were too many unpleasant thoughts waiting to crowd in. She got up and began putting things away. There were always things that needed to be put away and action helped a little.

Her scooping and shuffling of various possessions brought to light a newspaper dated earlier in the summer. It was the paper which contained her article. She gave up her tidying

efforts and carried it over to the bed. It was painful to remember that she had hoped to read her piece again happily
—as editor of the *Wand*. But perhaps reading it again would
clear up some of her muddle.

She had believed those words when she had set them
down. Words that presented America as a country of equal
opportunity for all; a country where every man could stand
beside every other man and be judged on his own merits—
not by his religion or the color of his skin. In that America
Mary Evans, who had made the most consistent contributions
to the *Wand,* had every right to be its editor.

But that doesn't make me like her any better, Val thought.
And it was mean of that little Negro girl to push Debby and
hurt her.

It was also mean of Hank Millard to throw a stone
through the window of one of those houses.

Until now she'd never thought much about all this, one
way or another. And she didn't want to face it now. She
didn't want to take sides and get into some sort of miserable
squabble. It wasn't her problem. Maybe it would clear up,
somehow.

She began to read slowly through the words she had
written, but once when she glanced across the room at her
own image in the mirror, she saw just such a quirk of worry
between her brows as her mother had begun to wear lately.

CHAPTER 8

INVITATION FROM TONY

Miss Kay called an assembly twenty minutes before lunch period the next day. Val, pushing along through the crowd, with Judy clinging to one arm, found Tony and Steve coming along on the other side.

It was odd the way those two seemed to like each other, when they were so very different. Certainly Tony had no interest in the literary matters that might interest Steve, but there was a common bond when it came to basketball. And Tony *was* likable, while Steve seemed to have a quiet knack for fitting himself in anywhere.

Val had been a little afraid that Tony might reproach her for running off so quickly yesterday when he'd said he would stay around to hear the result of her interview with Miss Kay. But if he had been annoyed, he had apparently forgotten about it now. Perhaps he hadn't waited for her after all.

Steve and Tony took seats next to them and Judy started wriggling about right away so that she could see in four directions at practically the same time.

"I wonder what this little gathering is all about?" she asked of nobody in particular.

Tony leaned past Steve. "Kay's going to make an announcement. Dad told me to watch and see how she handled it."

The auditorium was filling up now, buzzing with laughter and chattering voices. Then Miss Kay walked out on the stage and everyone stilled.

"I have an announcement to make," the principal said crisply and Tony gave them an I-told-you-so-look. "Mrs. Manning, president of the Willow Hill Woman's Club has asked me to let you know that a rally is to be held tonight at eight o'clock in the Town Hall auditorium. Mr. Wayne Millard will be the main speaker and you are requested to ask your mothers and fathers to attend. Young people are invited, too, so those of you who care to come will be welcome."

Miss Kay glanced at the paper in her hand and then went on.

"It is to be a citizens' meeting in which various urgent town matters will be discussed."

Val found herself wondering whether Miss Kay knew the real meaning behind this rally. Mrs. Manning had certainly let no grass grow under her feet.

Miss Kay folded the paper in her hands and refolded it. Her voice as she continued was quiet and unemotional, but you could hear every clipped word clearly.

"In the coming weeks Willow High School is going to be faced with a problem in Americanism. How we rise to the challenge, how we meet it, how we solve it, will show just what kind of people we are—not just what kind of Americans, but what kind of world citizens—and that is even more important than being an American."

The auditorium was completely still, but it seemed to Val

that there was something uneasy, uncomfortable about the stillness. Others had heard talk in their homes, just as she had, and the uneasiness she felt in herself was present in others too.

"As you know—" Miss Kay's voice held them, "—vans are bringing the possessions of new families into the housing project at the foot of the hill. A few of those families are already moving in and there will be many more in the weeks to come. We have had a few Negro students in our classes in the past and we have enjoyed having them here. We have been proud of Mary Evans' honors in scholarship and we know she is going to do a fine job as editor of the *Wand*."

A faint rustle ran through the crowd and Val's cheeks burned as she felt eyes turned her way. She fixed her gaze unwaveringly on the stage, pretending to be unaware of the curious glances.

Miss Kay's voice went on, quieting the rustle. "A great many of these young people will be coming to Willow High in the next few weeks and I hope we will make the best possible use of this opportunity to prove we can *live* the democracy we say we believe in."

Everyone applauded and the music director got up to lead them in songs; *America the Beautiful* and other patriotic numbers.

As they filed up the aisle afterwards Tony came between Judy and Val. "Kay is sure sticking her neck out. Looks like she'd better watch her step if she doesn't want to get in bad with this town."

"I think she was swell!" Judy said loyally. "That's the kind of talk we need if we're going to make things work out in this school. Don't you think so, Steve?"

"Sure," Steve said, "that's one of the things we need."

Tony was good-natured but derisive. "A couple more off the track! You'll get straightened out after a while. What about you, Val?"

That was putting it up to her. Putting up to her just what she wanted most to avoid—the necessity of taking sides. Someone came along just then and jostled the books she was carrying out of her arm and she was glad to drop them. Steve, who was nearest, helped her gather up her scattered possessions, and by the time they were collected Judy and Tony had gone on, arguing furiously.

She hoped she had side-stepped the question, but she knew when she reached her locker that Tony was still on the same subject. Judy had evidently rubbed him the wrong way and he was looking for someone to side in with him.

"Val's got more sense than to believe stuff like that," he said as she came up. "I'll bet she isn't happy about having Mary in as editor of the *Wand*. Are you, Val?"

It was perfectly true she wasn't. She shook her head without answering.

"See?" he challenged Judy, but she only put her nose in the air and turned away. That wasn't very smart of her, Val thought, if she wanted Tony to like her.

Tony leaned a shoulder against the locker next to Val's, ignoring Judy. "I want to talk to you. This rally Mrs. Manning and Dad are running tonight—you going?"

"I guess I'll have to," Val said. "Mother's on a committee or something. She'd probably have a fit if I stayed home."

Tony grinned understandingly. "That's the way it is with me, too. So how about going with me? Suppose I come over for you around ten to eight?"

Tony Millard had asked her for a date! *Tony Millard.*
Never mind if it was some sort of dull affair she didn't care
about—it was still a date. But there was Judy. Judy had first
claim, and she couldn't cut in on her best friend. She had to
say "no" quickly.

"I—I guess I'll be going with the whole family," she told
him. "I mean—" but she didn't really know what she meant,
so she couldn't finish the sentence.

"Okay," he said. "I'll come over and go with the whole
family, too. But I might be a little late. Maybe the whole
family won't want to wait for me."

"I'll wait for you," she said and turned hastily to open her
locker.

She heard him walk away and then felt Judy tugging at
her elbow. How much had Judy heard?

"Aren't you *ever* coming to lunch?" Judy sounded impa-
tient, but not angry.

All the way down to the lunchroom Val worried. She *had*
tried to get out of going with him. She hadn't meant to cut
in on Judy. Tony had done this of his own accord and, after
all, he could go out with anyone he pleased. She couldn't
have helped herself if she'd wanted to. Or could she?

They lined up with their trays, oblivious to the deafening
hubbub of the lunchroom as it closed in around them.

"Since when have you taken to eating anything as healthy
as spinach?" Judy demanded and Val looked in surprise at
the stringy green stuff in a saucer on her tray.

Judy's laughter was teasing. "It must be love if you don't
even know when you're eating spinach! Who's the lucky
guy?"

Val felt her cheeks burning, but she offered no defense.

Had Judy said that deliberately, or was it just one of her wise-cracking remarks?

"Look," Judy said, "there's Mary and no one's at the table with her. Let's go over and keep her company."

Mary Evans was the last person she wanted to talk to at that moment. Besides Tony and some of his gang were just getting into the chow line. She wouldn't be in his good graces long if she sat down at a table with Mary.

"I think Mary likes to eat alone," she offered lamely. "She never eats with the rest of us."

"Maybe that's our fault," Judy said. "Anyway, after that pep talk Miss Kay just handed out, we can't have Mary sitting at an empty table. Come along."

Again she could feel that miserable pull in two directions. She wanted to be nice to Mary—that was part of being a good sport. But just the same— She made up her mind abruptly and put her tray down at a nearby table, slid into a chair. Judy hesitated a moment and then joined her.

"You could have gone," Val said in a low voice.

Judy set her glass of milk down with a thump that sent liquid spilling over the brim. "Do you think I'd hurt her feelings that way? She saw us come in together. If I went over to her table alone she'd know it was because you wouldn't come with me."

"Then it's better this way," Val said. "Oh, Judy, I get so mixed up. How can you be so sure about what you think after what happened to Debby the other day? I should think that would have made you furious."

Judy started in on her lemon cream pie—her usual manner of procedure when no restraining elders were around.

"I guess I was mad," she said. "I'd have been mad at any

kid who hurt Debby. But I don't feel like being mad at all
Negroes just because of that. Anyway, cheer up. You going
to this talkathon tonight?"

"I have to."

"Then I expect I might as well go, too. I'll come around
for you early and we'll—"

So she didn't know. She hadn't overheard.

"I'm going with Tony," Val said in a low voice.

There was a silence during which Val ate spinach that
nearly choked her and avoided looking at Judy. Anyway it
was out. She wasn't sneaking around doing things behind
anyone's back.

Judy took another oversized mouthful of lemon cream pie
and recovered her voice without waiting to swallow the bite
of pie.

"A date with Tony Millard and the woman is practically
weeping into her spinach! No wonder you need vitamins.
What're you going to wear?"

Val wanted to hug her. If Judy could take it that way her
heart surely wasn't broken very badly.

"I don't know," Val said. "My green skirt, maybe. I got
spots on my blue one and forgot to take it to the cleaner's."

"You can borrow my yellow sweater," Judy offered.
"Mother just washed it and it looks like canary feathers."

Thinking about the yellow sweater helped. And if Judy
could offer her that she really couldn't care. Yellow would
be good with her dark coloring. For once in her life she just
had to look special.

"And I'll borrow mother's yellow flower for your hair,"
Judy went on, rising to the next level of generosity which

always resulted in farming out things that didn't belong to her.

Maybe life wasn't going to be so difficult after all. If Judy didn't mind whether or not she went out with Tony, and Tony was even mildly interested in Val Coleman—then perhaps tonight might be pretty nice. She wished they were going to a movie instead of the rally. But if she could go to the meeting and close her attention to everything unpleasant —just keep her mind on being with Tony. . . . That was the answer and she'd manage it somehow.

Maybe there were things in the world no one could help. So it wasn't any use being unhappy about them. It was better to think about pleasant things and from now on that was what she was going to do.

Having made her decision, she wondered why she couldn't feel more contented about it.

CHAPTER 9

VAL TAKES SIDES

Except for the creak of the porch swing, the night was very still. Her mother had left the porch light on when she and the others had gone off to the meeting, but as soon as they were out of sight Val had turned it off.

It was nicer to wait in the soft darkness, with only the light of a street lamp adding a faint illumination. She was glad Tony was late.

This was a real September night, with a briskness to the air that made Judy's yellow sweater feel good. Across the street somebody had been burning leaves and you could smell the smoke. A cheerful fall smell.

She put up her hand to touch the yellow flower in her hair. It wasn't Mrs. Piper's flower after all, but Mrs. Coleman's.

Her mother had come in while she was dressing and she'd liked the yellow sweater, though not the fact that Val had borrowed it. But she had once more been distressed about her daughter's hair.

Val had been happy when her mother put down her bag and gloves and picked up a comb. Her hands were so pretty and quick and clever, but for all their fluffing efforts, Val's hair went its own undistinguished way. Finally she had run off to her own room and come back with a spray of yellow jonquils that always looked lovely in her own hair. The effect wasn't quite the same with Val, but she felt it helped, and it had been nice to be fussed over. At the last minute her mother had even sprayed on a bit of her favorite perfume and Val sniffed herself happily now and pushed the swing back and forth with one toe.

Tony was awfully late. If he didn't get here soon they'd never be on time for the meeting and her mother would fret about that. Val didn't want to disappoint her so soon after she'd been so sweet and helpful.

Then she heard his car at the curb, heard the door open, and there he was, standing on the steps peering at her through the dim light. "Hi, toots! Ready to go?"

Even though she knew it was late and they'd have to hurry, she almost hoped that he'd come up on the porch and sit in the swing for a few minutes. But he stood on the steps, waiting for her. She slipped past him and went toward the car a little breathlessly. She ought to say something, but she couldn't think of anything clever to say. So she said the first thing that came to mind—the worst possible choice she could have made.

"I was afraid you'd never get here," she told him. "If we don't hurry we'll be late."

He didn't hurry after her, but at least he came, swinging along lazily until he was beside her, as if he had all the time in the world. The car door was swinging carelessly open as he had left it and when she came under the street light to get in, he gave a low whistle.

"Pretty slick tonight," he said. "I like that sweater."

She got into the wonderful red car, feeling very special
indeed.

It took only a minute or two to cover the distance to the
Town Hall from Val's house. They could have walked it
easily, but it was much more impressive to drive up in
Tony's car. She was sorry everyone was inside so that her
dramatic arrival couldn't be noted.

They could hear the crowd singing the *Star Spangled Ban-
ner* as they neared the steps and Val started to hurry.

"Take it easy," Tony said. "Let 'em get past the Pledge
before we go in."

The singing finished as they entered the hallway and she
and Tony stood outside the auditorium door while the sing-
song voices recited the *Pledge to the Flag*. Then everyone sat
down with a great creaking of chairs and Tony and Val
slipped into seats at the rear of the hall. Willow Hill was
proud of this Town Hall building, put up before the war,
and of the fine auditorium that was as good or better than
any theater.

Mrs. Manning stood behind the speaker's rostrum, looking
like a rather large gray pigeon. She was very poised, very
sure of herself.

Several important personages sat on the platform behind
the rostrum, with Wayne Millard in the center. They made
an imposing pair, Mrs. Manning and Mr. Millard. Both
figures of civic justice, large and important and worthy.
Though as far as appearance went, Val preferred Mr. Millard.

It was easy to see why Tony admired his father so much.
He was a big, handsome man, with a head of graying hair
that gave him a distinguished look. He still carried an ath-

letic stamp and you could imagine what trouble he must
have made for opposing football teams when he was younger.

Mrs. Manning was greeting the audience, and Val looked
around for her own family. There was Nick, halfway down,
slumped in his favorite position, though for once he couldn't
plant his feet higher than his head. Mrs. Coleman sat next to
him, her head held high, though Val suspected that that nervous frown was still between her brows. Judy sat next to her
—you could spot her red topknot anywhere—and then came
Steve. Apparently the Pipers had not come. Mrs. Piper, as
Mrs. Coleman often regretted, was one of the least civic-
minded women in town and her husband hated meetings.

Val's eyes moved on. Not many of the kids from school had
come, though there were a few here with their parents. But
the auditorium was well filled. The Woman's Club must
have worked fast and put on a lot of pressure to turn out a
crowd like this. Or had these people come because most of
the town was as stirred up as the leaders about the housing
project?

But that was the sort of thing she didn't want to think
about tonight. Here she was on a date with Tony Millard.
That was what she wanted to remember.

Some rows ahead a single vacant seat caught her attention.
It was odd, since the place was well filled, that a seat as far
down as that should be empty. And then she saw the reason.

At the end of the row, beyond the empty seat, a man sat
alone. He was a big man, lean and solid looking, and he sat
very erect and proud, his eyes fixed unswervingly on the
platform as if he were unaware of the empty seat next to him.

"Good gosh!" Tony said. "Look at that. How'd he get in?"

The man turned his head to look across the auditorium and Val recognized him.

"Isn't that Mary Evans' father?" she asked. "He's a minister, isn't he?"

"Dr. Evans? Sure that's who it is. Minister or not, he's got a heck of a lot of nerve to show up here."

But it must have taken courage too, as well as nerve, Val thought, to come where he knew so many would be against him.

"He's probably here to make trouble," Tony said. "Watch and see."

Val sank back in her seat. It was going to be harder than she expected to keep her mind on pleasant things tonight. Somehow the sight of one person standing up against many always made her want to be on the side of the one. Whether he was right or not. And that wasn't very sensible.

Up on the stage Mrs. Manning was speaking eloquently of things they all loved. Their homes and shady streets, the great willows that gave the town its name, their history dating back to the Indian Wars. Their lives bound up in this town and the future they planned for their children. It was a story to make her listeners swell with pride and the sense of "belonging." There was nothing argumentative in her words. Everything was sweetness and light.

But now she was coming to the point.

"We are faced with a problem tonight," she went on, "that has serious implications for everything we hold dear. We have all seen blighted areas where the homes, streets and people typify another way of life. In nearby cities there are such areas as you all have seen. You would not move into them. But they can move in on you. In this town we are now faced with such a problem."

Val could sense the stiffening that ran through the audience, the alertness of attention.

"Communities," Mrs. Manning said, "are really the people who live in them. If you took out all the people who live here and substituted those from another town, it wouldn't be the same. We wouldn't see the same familiar faces on the streets. Our institutions would change, our schools, our churches. Isn't it easy to see that the change might be for the worse and that we might not wish to live here any more?

"Now, by the decision of people who do not live here, we are to be subjected to a large scale invasion of Negroes. Many of us feel that the damage that will be done to all of us is too great to suffer in silence and without complaint. Many of us feel steps should be taken to prevent this proposal from going any further. So this evening we are met to consider practical means of reversing this plan. That the town is behind us is evidenced by the very size of this audience. It is evidenced by the high standing in the community of those appearing on this platform. Tonight we want you to listen to a man who has long been identified with public interest in Willow Hill. That he is public spirited is above question. He is raising his family in this town, he is a church member, and a successful business man in this community. I want to present Mr. Wayne Millard."

Wayne Millard knew audiences. You could tell it by the way he looked around, waiting, confident of his ability to command absolute silence. When that silence was his he began to speak in a friendly, natural fashion. He leaned on the rostrum informally—the good neighbor stepping down among his friends and speaking as one of them.

He mentioned how hard Mrs. Manning had worked to get this meeting together, and of her efforts in behalf of the community. He had, he said, been reluctant to accept her invitation to speak here tonight because, even though he had the deepest convictions on the matter, and the gravest concern, he felt his reactions should not be used to sway others.

Listening, Val thought, "He doesn't mean that. He's *here* to sway others."

But eventually, he went on, he could no longer close his eyes to the fact that scores, even hundreds of others, felt as he did. This must be stopped!

"What Mrs. Manning did not go into," he pointed out, "was the specific effects this project would have on our community. It will depress property values. When Negroes move into a neighborhood property values go plunging down. If enough move in they can take over very sound homes, like yours and mine, for less than the mortgage value. Why? Because white purchasers will not buy into a Negro district. The houses you saved to buy cannot be sold except at a loss. Entire neighborhoods deteriorate."

His voice rang deep and vibrant, striking alarm into his listeners as he intended it to strike. Val felt a little frightened. If this was true, then the savings Nick had put into their house would be lost. Where would they go? How would they find money to buy another house somewhere else?

"Do you want this to happen?" The speaker's tone challenged his listeners. "How do *you* feel about it?"

Down near the front a man jumped up. "I'm practically across the street from this project and I don't like it. I've

got all my savings tied up in my home and I can see them
going out the window."

He would have continued, but another angry voice broke
in.

"I run a restaurant in that end of town and what am I
going to do about it if Negroes come in and want to be
served? I'll lose my white customers and then where'll I be?"

The audience was buzzing with excitement now. Everyone
seemed to want to put in his own two cents. A third man was
on his feet—a man Val recognized as owning a small store.

"It's an accepted fact," he said, "that the Negro and the
white man belong to two different species. It is our duty as
civilized human beings to help these people to the best of
our ability, to aid them to better ways of living. But we do
not have to accept them as equals."

Perhaps if Mary's father hadn't been there, Val could have
listened more easily. As it was, her sympathy kept going out
toward the single Negro in the audience. How did he feel
hearing that he belonged to a different species? Besides, *was*
it an accepted fact? Last year Miss Kay had told her classes
again and again that anthropologists had proved that the
superior race theory was a myth.

"We mean these people no harm." Mr. Millard was speaking again. "We wish them well in every respect. There is, I
know, not the slightest racial prejudice among us. But we
feel that the opening of this housing project in our community can cause nothing but ill-will on all sides. Surely
these people can have no wish to come where they are not
wanted. A grave mistake has been made and in order to
rectify it for the good of all, you and I will have to work
together."

Val stole a look at Tony. He was watching his father proudly. There were apparently two things Tony cared about most—sports and his father. It was a good thing neither love interfered with the other. If they ever did—poor Tony. But somehow she liked him all the better for being loyal. Only—she wished that squirmy feeling wouldn't come back as she listened to Mr. Millard. She couldn't see him with Tony's eyes and the things he was saying made her uncomfortable.

Others stood up, some rambling in their statements, some openly seething with the prejudice Mr. Millard had said did not exist among them, others more cautious, though willing to follow a concerted lead. But all sincere, all believing Mr. Millard's viewpoint was right.

There seemed to be a strong representation from the west side of town, Val noted. Property values weren't any too high over there, and some of the boys from that section had a reputation for being tough. More than once they'd been trouble makers in school.

Wasn't there anyone who could speak for the other side? Val glanced at the faces around her, but most of them looked concerned or indignant. Except for one big man at the end of her row. She recognized him with interest. That was Jonathan Kincaid, owner of Willow Hill's biggest drugstore. And he was president of the school board, too. He had always seemed a frightening sort of person to Val because of something that had happened when she was a little girl.

She couldn't have been more than five the time her mother had taken her downtown to his drugstore and Mr. Kincaid had come out from behind the counter. He had been big and terrifying and he had boomed at her with the most enormous voice Val had ever heard. She had burst into shrieks of fright and her mother had had to take her out of the store. That memory persisted and she had never quite gotten over her fear of him.

But now, though he was wearing a tremendous frown between bushy brows, she had a feeling that he was not frowning about property losses or in sympathy with what Mr. Millard was saying. As she watched, wondering what he was thinking, he stood up big and towering. When he spoke his voice had the booming tone she remembered.

"Wait a minute now," he said. "I know all you good people have the interest of Willow Hill at heart. So have I. But suppose we stop thinking about property values for a couple of minutes and think about human values. How about it—which is more important?"

But Mr. Millard did not mean to be caught on anything like that. He smiled jovially as if the drugstore owner had said something very funny, and tossed the question into the lap of the audience.

"Our good friend Jonathan Kincaid wants to know which is more important—human values or property values. Maybe he's overlooked the way the two are pretty much mixed up. I have a couple of boys and a wife. They're *my* human values. Think I want to see them left in the lurch because a housing project happened to open up in this town? Maybe some of the rest of you have human values like that, too. What do you think? Do you want to see those you love provided for, or do you want to see them lose out on everything you've worked all your life to build up?"

A mutter of voices gave them his answer and Jonathan Kincaid sat down, still frowning. But now another man had risen in the audience and Val was aware of the way Tony stiffened in the seat beside her.

"See," he whispered. "Trouble's coming. What'd I tell you?"

There was sudden quiet all over the hall, but it was an ominous sort of quiet, with complete attention focused on the man who stood facing the stage.

"Will you allow a Negro to speak?" Dr. Evans asked.

Some one broke the silence with a boo and Mrs. Manning rapped her gavel sharply. Tony's father looked down at him, friendly and smiling.

"Go ahead, Joe. We believe in freedom of speech for everybody."

By so little a thing as a name Wayne Millard had lessened the man's dignity. By omitting the courtesy of a title he had set him aside as an inferior.

Dr. Evans bowed his head courteously. There was nothing aggressive about his manner, but there was no timidity in him either. He must have known that he spoke to a group that was against him before he opened his mouth, yet he showed no hesitancy, did not falter. Watching him, Val felt a surge of admiration go through her. It *did* take courage to stand up like that, knowing before you started that you didn't have a chance, but going ahead anyway. And then, as he began to speak, Val saw that it would take more than the carelessly insulting use of a name to injure his pride of bearing.

"My people are deeply concerned in this matter, too," he said. "For many of us these houses offer the first decent living quarters we have ever had. I know some of the families who are moving into them. I know they want only to fit in as quietly as possible and to be as good citizens as you will allow them to be. Why not give them a chance?"

There was an uncomfortable silence in the hall. Everybody in town knew Dr. Evans. The way he worked to help his people was common knowledge. No one wanted to hurt *him*. Mr. Millard continued to smile down at him and he spoke in a kindly enough tone.

"If all your people were like you, Joe, it might be a different story. But we know they're not, and you know they're not. They've had their chances over and over again—and what do they do with them? Walk through the Negro section of any American town and you'll see."

Dr. Evans answered him quietly. "I wonder if this audience realizes that the houses we are permitted to move into in any town are always those in so deteriorated a condition that landlords have given up trying to repair them. These buildings are sold or rented to Negroes at such exorbitant prices that it is necessary for several families to double up and live together. The rentals in this project will be moderate and such crowding will not be necessary."

But though the crowd was not against Dr. Evans himself, they didn't want to listen to him. Looking about her again Val saw only evidence of closed minds. These people knew what they *wanted* to think and they had no intention of being swayed off the course Wayne Millard had chosen for them. Their own close interests were being threatened, so what did they care about how Negroes lived? After all, every man had to think of his own family first.

Dr. Evans seemed to sense the fact that he was defeated, but he stood where he was a moment longer.

"There's just one thing more I want to say." There was

such deep sorrow in his voice that something ached in Val's throat as she listened. "People working together can split this town into two camps hating each other, bringing misery to all. Or people—all kinds of people working together—can build it into a better town than it's ever been before."

He stepped into the aisle and walked slowly toward the rear of the hall. No one booed now. No one laughed or jeered. The doors at the end of the aisle swung shut behind him and a sigh went through the audience. The hall rustled with whispering. Every man was nudging his neighbor to get his reaction.

Val glanced at Tony. He was not looking her way, but staring at the back of the seat before him. He looked as if something which didn't belong there and which he didn't know what to do with had got tangled in the machinery of his thinking.

Then Wayne Millard's voice called him back. "Doc Evans is okay. We all know that. We've got nothing against him. But we can't expect him to see this the way we do. The people moving in on this town won't be like him. Now then— here's what we have to do—"

He had them again. If for an instant a faint doubt had swept the good people of Willow Hill, it was gone as they listened to their leader. Tony straightened in his seat and glanced at Val.

"You see? I told you he'd try to make trouble. But leave it to dad to straighten things out."

Val looked away without answering. More than anything in the world she wanted to get out of this hall. She didn't want to listen to the plans and discussion that were going on. She wanted to get out in the air where she could breathe again.

Eventually the meeting broke up and the moment she was able to Val left her seat. She and Tony moved with the tide, carried along toward the auditorium doors. And suddenly she knew that she couldn't wait for him to take her home. She had to get away by herself.

She put her hand on his arm. "I know you'll want to go home with your father. Thank you for bringing me, but I'll just wait in the hall for my folks. Don't worry about me."

She gave him no chance to protest, but slipped into the crowd and allowed it to separate them. Perhaps this wasn't the way to treat him, but there was no other choice at the moment. Later she would try to make him understand. She had no desire to wait for her mother either and listen to more of what Mrs. Manning had said.

On her way out she glimpsed Miss Kay standing over near the wall, looking troubled and unhappy. Obviously she wasn't in sympathy with the Millard crowd and Val wished she could go over to talk to her. But when she looked again, the crowd had cut in and the principal was gone.

Outside the night air felt wonderful against her hot face. Clean and fresh and free. She walked along quickly, afraid someone would stop to talk to her. She wanted to get away to the pleasant little streets of Willow Hill. Out into darkness where the only sound was the rustle of a September breeze through fading leaves.

She knew now why she had to be alone. She had to be alone so that she could make up her mind. People could go along for a time playing ostrich, pretending there wasn't really any trouble, but sooner or later the moment came when you had to take sides. She had to choose now for once and for all. Was she to side with Tony and his father? With her mother and Mrs. Manning?

She walked more slowly now, aware of the little streets, dipping toward the hill. They looked just as they always did. Lamplight glowed at the windows and people sat in easy chairs reading. Not all of Willow Hill had been at the meeting.

These streets were America. America the beautiful. "To crown thy good with brotherhood—" That was the way it ought to be. The way it could be. "One nation indivisible, with liberty and justice for all." Those words didn't mean "liberty and justice for *me,* but not for the other fellow."

She heard footsteps behind her, but she did not look up. Let whoever it was pass her by. If she didn't look around, perhaps she wouldn't need to speak. But the steps fitted into the pattern of her own. Tony? Oh, she hoped it wasn't Tony.

"This isn't the way home," Steve said. "Where are you going?"

She glanced up, startled. She hadn't known her feet were taking her in this direction. Or why. And then, as Steve's stride matched the rhythm of her own, she knew where she was going. Knew simply and suddenly without hesitation. Her choice had been made. She knew which side she was on.

"I want to find out where Mary Evans lives," she said. "I want to tell her I'd like to be her associate editor on the *Wand.* I want to tell her tonight."

CHAPTER 10

MARY EVANS

The Negro section of town lay on the far side of the hill, nowhere near the housing project. There had been no room in that crowded section to put new buildings.

Val walked along briskly with Steve beside her. He had said nothing at all to the announcement of her intention and she was a little disappointed. Somehow she'd wanted him to approve what she was doing.

"What will your mother say about this?" he asked after they'd walked a block in silence.

She shrugged. Now that she'd made her decision, now that she was no longer pulled two ways, she felt buoyant, even a little reckless.

"I don't know!" she cried. "I don't even care. All I know is that I have to do this. That is what I want to do."

"What if Mary Evans doesn't want your help?"

She thought about that, remembering the exultant triumph in Mary's eyes when the appointment had come to her, remembering that later moment in Miss Kay's office when she had been sure that Mary's quiet acceptance of Miss Kay's suggestion that Val have a place on the staff had been sham. But things were different now. Val Coleman was

different. Mary would know she truly and sincerely wanted
to help.

"I think it will be all right," she told Steve. "After all, she
really will need my help. And if she knows I'd like to give
it—"

She let the sentence go unfinished and Steve made no
comment. He was evidently reserving his decision till later,
and that worried her a little.

The neat rows of modern houses had ended, falling off
into ramshackle buildings with narrow porches and broken,
unpainted railings. But yellow light glowed at the window of
a house they were passing and a Negro woman sat near a
lamp, sewing. Somehow there was a sense of a pattern repeated for Val, a sameness to the scene. Lamplight and a
woman near a window. Not black or white. Just a woman
sitting by a window. Any woman anywhere.

Steve looked about for someone to ask for directions. On
the other side of the street a boy knelt in the light from a
street lamp. His back was toward them and he bent over
something that whimpered in his arms. They went across
and he looked up as they stopped beside him. It was Jeff
Evans and the whimpering creature was a small brown dog.

Jeff recognized them without surprise, but he had no smile
for them this time. All his concerned attention was focused
on the dog.

"Look at that," he said. "He's got his paw hurt bad.
Smashed it somehow."

Steve bent closer to see. "Better watch it. When they're
hurt like that they can bite without meaning to."

"I know." Jeff held one hand up to the light and Val saw

a jagged scar along the wrist. "I've gotten bit before. I guess
I'd bite too, if I was hurt like that."

"We were looking for your sister," Val said. "Do you live
around here?"

Jeff nodded in the direction of the next block. "Sure.
Right down there. The place over the grocery store. I'd go
along and show you, but I have to get this fellow quiet first.
He has to trust me better before he'll let me carry him."

They left him murmuring softly to the dog and walked
toward the grocery store. At one side was an open door at the
foot of a narrow flight of stairs. They went into the small
square of hallway and rang the bell at the bottom of the
stairs, but for a moment nothing happened. Then, as they
waited, wondering what to do next, a little girl came dashing full tilt down the steep flight, with only the banister to
save her from tumbling.

Val recognized her as the vindictive child who had pushed
Debby down in the dust. But there was nothing angry about
her now. She was laughing as she came and her black pig-
tails, ending in neat red ribbons, danced upon her shoulders.
From the dimly lighted hall above a woman's voice called
down.

"Patty-Lou, you come right back here this minute. Your
bath's ready and you're up too late now."

"I ain't gonna have no bath!" the child called back to the
woman on the floor above.

"Don't say 'ain't gonna,'" the voice of authority corrected,
"and come back here right this minute!"

Just as the little thing was about to fly out the door, Steve
caught her and held on tight.

"Maybe we can help," Steve said. "We seem to have made a capture down here."

The little girl squirmed about in his grasp to look up at him with big, astonished eyes. Then she began to fight and claw furiously.

The woman—she was hardly more than a girl—came quickly down the stairs and Val had again a brief sense of a familiar scene repeated. How many times Mrs. Piper or Judy chased Debby and Binx at bath time. And always with a cheerful scolding that took time out to correct grammar, even in the middle of discipline. Except that Debby wasn't the spitfire this child appeared to be.

The girl took the struggling child off Steve's hands. "Patty-Lou, behave! Nobody's going to hurt you." She turned apologetically to the visitors. "I'm sorry. She—she doesn't like strangers. I didn't know anyone was down here. Are you looking for someone?"

"Mary Evans," Val told her quickly. "Does she live here?"

"She's my sister-in-law," the girl said. "I'll tell her you're here."

She ran back upstairs with the child unprotestingly in tow. A moment later Mary came to the head of the stairs. If she felt surprise at sight of her company, she did not betray it.

"Please come up," she said and waited for them at the head of the stairs.

The upper hallway was dingy and dim, but a patch of light showed at one end and Mary led the way into a crowded little room at the front of the building. It was a neat room, and very clean, but the furniture was old and worn and over near one window a cot had been made up. That was for Jeff, probably. Evidently he had moved in with his family without waiting till they could get into a project house.

Val seated herself on the couch Mary indicated, with Steve beside her, feeling awkward and ill-at-ease. If Mary would just be a little more cordial, this would be easier. But Mary, though polite, was as guarded as ever in her manner. She was waiting to learn her visitors' business and there was none of Jeff's easy friendliness in her manner.

Val's glance went helplessly about the room, searching for some means she could use to break the ice. Her attention was halted by a row of pictures along one wall. They were apparently fashion designs done in water color, all by the same artist.

"How interesting," Val cried. "Do you mind if I look?"

Mary offered no objection and Val crossed the room to stand before the row of pictures. They were really good—nicely drawn and with a touch of originality about them. The figures were languid and long-limbed, and the dresses they wore were well cut, with interesting detail in the design and really lovely color. At the corner of each drawing a name was sketched in boldly: "Mava."

Val turned back to Mary. "Whoever Mava is, she's good. These are wonderful."

There was the faintest softening in Mary's expression. "I'm Mava. I mixed up some of the letters in my name. I thought it might make a good name for a designer."

"It's perfect. But I didn't know you wanted to be a dress designer. I thought—well, your writing for the *Wand*—"

"I like to write," Mary said, "but it's not my main ambition. Someday I'm going to design dresses that will be seen on Park Avenue and Hollywood Boulevard."

There was an odd intenseness in her tone and Val knew she had not spoken the words in any sense of bragging. It was as if she were promising herself something with all the determination in her.

"I suppose you think an ambition like that is silly," Mary said. The softening had gone out of her face and her tone was cold, unfriendly.

"Why should I think it silly? When you have talent like that—"

Mary did not answer her directly. Her guard was safely up again. "You wanted to talk to me?" she asked.

Val glanced uneasily at Steve. He had known this would not be as easy as she thought, and somehow the brief interlude of talk about the pictures had made it more difficult than ever.

"There was a meeting tonight in the Town Hall," Val began. "Maybe you know?"

The Negro girl seemed to stiffen even more in her manner. "Yes," she said, "I know."

It was hard for Val to go on because a new understanding was sharp in her mind. She wanted to describe the meeting, to tell Mary how Dr. Evans had stood courageously up to Wayne Millard. But now it was as if she could feel with her own sensibilities exactly what it might be like to sit alone in an auditorium of white people, aware that no one else would sit beside you because your skin was darker than theirs.

She knew with her own feelings what it might be like to be a brown girl in a school filled with white girls who forgot about you without intending to be cruel, not taking you into their activities because they never thought about you as being like themselves underneath your dark skin. For that queer, sharp moment it was as if she—Val Coleman, who knew perfectly well that she was just like anyone else—had suddenly had to meet on every hand looks that shut her out, that said, "You're different." Looks that said harder things than that: "Because you are a Negro you are stupid and ignorant and dirty and lazy and we don't want you here. You're not like us. How silly and pretentious for you to have an ambition to design dresses under the name of Mava. Negro girls don't do things like that."

Her sudden flash of insight made her understand that look of triumph Mary had worn when Miss Kay had appointed her editor. That was something few Negro girls achieved in any school. She had been triumphantly glad—not just for herself—but for all her people. What any Negro achieved must help all the others.

But somehow Val could not say any of these things to Mary Evans.

Steve came to her rescue. "We went to the meeting to-night and we thought we'd like to see what we could do to help counteract what Mr. Millard's crowd is trying to accomplish."

Val found her voice again. "I want to help on the *Wand.* I really want to, Mary. I don't care what position you give me, just so you'll let me help."

Mary's dark eyes turned her way, but there was no gentleness in them, no pleasure over the offer. "Miss Kay said you could be associate editor if you wanted to."

How could she reach the girl, Val wondered, a little annoyed now. Mary was completely indifferent to her offer and how could you help anyone who didn't want to be helped?

But before she could think of anything else to say, she heard the sound of feet on the stairs. Long legs, those must be, taking the steps two at a time.

The little girl's mother ran into the hall and they heard her eager words. "Jack, how did it come out?"

A man's voice answered. "I go to work tomorrow, Linda honey. Cub reporter and general handy man on the *Willow Hill News*. Not much money to start, but it's a swell opportunity. It's what I want to do."

Interest came to life in Mary's face. "That's my older brother. He's been overseas until a couple of months ago. Now that he's out of the Army it looked as if the only job open to him would be over at the Hubbard Plant. And he doesn't fit in there."

Jack and Linda came into the living room and Mary introduced them. A moment later Patty-Lou came running in, wrapped in a towel, to hear about the news. Her father caught the child up and held her against his shoulder, dampness and all.

"You'd better be impressed," Jack Evans told his daughter gayly. "I'm a newspaperman now."

Patty-Lou laughed happily, but her eyes were still upon the strangers. There was less antagonism in them now, as if her mother might have been talking to her back of the scenes. Her attention seemed particularly attracted by Val's borrowed yellow sweater. Debby liked to touch things, too, and when Patty-Lou put out a hand to the brightness, Val moved nearer.

"It feels like canary feathers, doesn't it?" she asked the little girl. "Not that I've ever felt canary feathers. Have you?"

Patty-Lou nodded solemnly. "Sure I have. Dickie over there."

She pointed toward the cage near a window and everyone laughed.

"Dickie is one of Jeff's lame ducks," Linda explained. "His owner thought he was going to die and gave him to Jeff and he nursed him back to very good health."

"We saw Jeff before we came up here," Steve said. "He was looking after a pup with a smashed paw."

"Another one!" Mary cried and there was something like despair in her tone. "He's not going to bring it here. I won't have it!"

"Let him be," Jack Evans said gently. "He cares about looking after sick animals as much as you care about drawing those dress pictures."

"And if we let him be what will happen?" Mary went on. "He'll grow up like Father. He'll spend his life taking care of animals instead of humans, but the animals won't pay any better than the humans do." She caught the look of surprise in Val's eyes and the storm went out of her. "I'm sorry. I didn't mean to parade the family skeleton. It's just that some-times I get so tired of—"

She stopped and Val saw the way she looked across the room to the row of pictures on the wall. It was as if she were promising herself something. Promising that someday things would be different for the Evans family because of the designs of a girl who called herself "Mava."

"Listen," Jack said. "There he is now." There was a note of anxiety in his tone and Val knew he didn't mean Jeff.

Someone else was coming up the stairs, someone whose steps plodded heavily in weariness and discouragement.

Linda glanced at Mary. "Do you suppose—?"

"I'm afraid so," Mary said.

The steps reached the head of the stairs, paused as if the climber must get his breath. Then they came slowly on and Mary's father came into the little room. He did not much resemble the man who had stood up to face Wayne Millard earlier in the evening. He looked older and more tired and worn.

"So you went to the meeting?" Mary said. "You promised you wouldn't. You knew it wouldn't do any good."

Dr. Evans looked about the room, his eyes questioningly on the two outsiders.

Mary spoke quickly. "This is Val Coleman. From school, you know. She—she's going to be associate editor on the *Wand.* And this is Stephen Reid."

His shoulders straightened as he acknowledged the introductions. Whatever his inner sense of defeat, this man would hide it from strangers.

"We heard you tonight," Steve said. "We thought you were fine."

Dr. Evans shook his head. "I'm afraid I did no good. But I felt someone had to speak for my people. I am glad to know there were two in the hall who were not against me."

"More than that," Steve told him. "The trouble is, it always seems to be the other kind that makes the most noise. The—the—"

"The haters," Val supplied. "But Mr. Kincaid wasn't against you and there must be others. I wonder if there's any way of finding them and getting them together?"

But no one seemed to have any ideas on that. Val stood up. "We'd better be getting along home. I just wanted to tell you

I'd like to help on the *Wand*, Mary. I didn't want to wait till tomorrow."

"Thank you," Mary said, but the chill was in her voice again and Val knew that the other girl was not convinced of her sincerity.

As they went out they could hear Patty-Lou's voice. "Mary, will you make me a yellow sweater to go with that pretty skirt you made for me? Will you, Mary? Yellow like canary feathers."

At the bottom of the stairs they met Jeff coming in. The hurt puppy was cradled trustfully in his arms and Jeff smiled as he stood against the wall to let them pass. He was still incurious about their visit, all his interest focused on the dog.

"I'm going to fix him up," he said. "He'll be all right."

"Sure he will," Steve said, and then they were outside again.

"Mary won't like that," Val said softly. "Isn't she a queer girl, Steve? Somehow you can't get at her."

"Maybe we seem queer to her, too. Rushing over to tell her you wanted to have that job on the *Wand*."

"I hadn't thought about it that way," Val said. "Maybe we all seem queer to people who don't understand what we do. But the Evanses are nice. I can't see where they'd make such terrible neighbors."

"I can't either," Steve said. "But take a look over there."

They were walking slowly down the next block beside a picket fence that had known better days. Overhead a street light stood ghostly in the moonlight, with no bulb burning because a stone had broken the globe. But that happened over in the better sections of town, too. There were always kids to whom a street lamp looked like a challenge and an invitation. However, that wasn't what Steve meant.

She looked across the fence to a rubbish-filled front porch that probably hadn't been swept in weeks, if ever. There were banana peels and eggshells in the weedy yard, all being pawed over by a whining, mangy dog.

"Ugh!" Val said. "I wouldn't want to live next door to people like that."

"Probably Mary's family wouldn't enjoy it either."

They walked along quietly, moving toward home.

"But, Steve," Val said after a while, "I'm getting all mixed up. Either Wayne Millard is wrong or he's right."

"I guess it's not as simple as that," Steve said. "I don't think a fellow's religion or the color of his skin has much to do with making him throw garbage out his window. Lots of very poor people live like that. There are plenty of white people you wouldn't want as neighbors."

"Well, then—why can't we get together somehow—people like mother and the Evanses and Mrs. Manning and the Millards and all work to educate people so they don't throw garbage out the window and—"

"Dad used to say it wasn't just education," Steve told her. "I guess it's more a matter of having something to hope for and live for and look forward to. When people get to feeling every hand is against them and they can barely earn enough to keep alive—they begin to feel defeated. And the defeated don't care. What difference does it make where the garbage goes or if the porch gets mended?"

"Mary won't take defeat," Val said.

"I don't think she will. But everyone isn't as strong and determined as Mary."

Val stole a side glance at Steve as they walked along. It was queer to remember that she'd thought him uninteresting at first glance.

She sighed. "You know so much. You always know the answers."

He laughed at that. "I don't know anything. It's just that these things were always coming up for discussion at home and I've heard a lot of talk about them. The trouble is, I don't know how you can do much when everybody jumps up and down and screeches that everybody else who is different is all wrong and shouldn't be allowed the same privileges that he has. . . ."

They walked home silently on that somber thought. When they reached the house the porch light was on, but the rooms were dark. That meant her mother wasn't home yet and her father had come in alone. Sometimes a committee meeting called at Mrs. Manning's request would keep her mother after the meeting proper had broken up. Probably that had happened tonight. In that case she preferred to have friends bring her home, rather than keep Nick waiting around for her.

Val stopped before they reached the front steps. "Thanks, Steve, for going down there with me tonight. I think Dad's around on the terrace. I'm going out to talk to him before mother comes home."

He understood. "Guess I'll go on to bed." He hesitated as if he wanted to say something more, but apparently the right words wouldn't come and he went into the house.

She followed the walk around, stepping carefully in the darkness. Nick was there in a big chair with his pipe. Val pulled a padded cushion out of another chair and dropped it close to his feet. Then she sat down and clasped her hands about her knees. He smoked in silence and for a moment it was almost like old times when they would sit together and not talk, not needing to talk because of the warm feeling of comradeship and understanding between them.

But there was a difference now and words were necessary. She hurried into them a little breathlessly.

"Steve and I have just been down to Mary Evans' house. I wanted to tell Mary that I'd be associate editor, or anything else she'd like to have me be on the *Wand*."

Nick puffed at his pipe and waited. Val tried to see his face, but it was only a hazy outline in the darkness.

"I had to, Nick," she said. "I had to!"

His hands found hers where they were clasped against her knees and gave them a little squeeze. "So you've picked sides, have you? Your mother will be upset about this, you know."

"I know," she said. She wished she could talk to him. She wished she could find out what he was thinking. "Did you know that Negro who spoke at the meeting tonight was Mary's father?" she asked.

"Dr. Evans?" Nick said. "Yes, I know him. A swell guy. Does a lot for his people. But he's apt to give away more than he can afford and his own family finds it tough going sometimes. Speaking up tonight took guts."

"I wonder how you get to—to have guts?"

Nick chuckled. "That's not a word your mother would exactly approve. Better not go tossing it around."

"It's a good word," Val said, "and I want to know."

Nick thought a while. "Mostly it seems to be something people have when they are kids and then grow out of later on

"But why?" Val asked. "Why do people have to grow out of it."

"I don't know. I suppose they get afraid of things. Afraid of losing their jobs. Afraid of being different from the pack. Afraid of saying what they believe because the consequences can be pretty uncomfortable."

"But the haters aren't afraid. They talk up. They get things their way. Mr. Millard and Mrs. Manning and people like that."

"I know."

"But I want to *do* something!" Val cried. "Somewhere in this town there must be people who really believe in the things they teach us in school."

"Maybe you're a hater, too," Nick said.

She started to protest indignantly, but he patted her hand.

"Just so it's injustice you hate, honey. People who push other people around because of their own selfishness. Go on hating it all your life. Don't give up somewhere along the line and stand by because that's the easiest thing to do."

He'd never talked to her like this before. She hadn't known he felt as strongly about it as this. She wanted now to tell him about the Evanses—about Jack's new job, and about Linda and little Patty-Lou, who could be as sweet as Debby when she wasn't angry and fighting something other people couldn't see. But she heard the front door open and close and the familiar sound of her mother's heels clicking down the hall.

"Well, kid, this is it," Nick said. "Maybe we'd better go in."

Mrs. Coleman was in the living room, spreading out papers on the piano. The nervous little frown she so often wore lately marred a forehead that could be so smooth and pretty when she was unworried.

"Hello," she said as her husband and daughter came in. "What did you think of the meeting? Mrs. Manning and Mr. Millard feel that it was very successful."

"Do you really want to know what we think of it, or is that just a rhetorical question?" Nick asked.

The frown deepened. "Oh, Nick! I hoped that when you heard the good sense spoken there tonight you'd change your attitude."

"There was good sense spoken all right," Nick said. "Two men spoke it—Jonathan Kincaid and Joseph Evans."

"Nick! Mrs. Manning says they meant well, but that was all sentimental idealism. We have to be realistic."

Nick shrugged and went over to his favorite chair to pick up a new detective story and settle down with his pipe. Now the field was hers, Val thought with a sinking feeling.

"Mother," she said, "I'd like to talk to you about something."

Mrs. Coleman rubbed her fingertips across her forehead, "Please dear, not now. I'm very tired. Mrs. Manning has put quite a lot of work into my hands and I have to think about it."

"Mother—" it was hard to stand her ground, but she managed it. "Mother, it's very important."

Mrs. Coleman looked up from her papers and despair came into her face. "Oh, Val! The yellow flower I loaned you—I do hope you haven't lost it."

Val's hand flew to the place where the flower had been, but it was gone. And she'd never noticed. She hadn't the faintest idea where she might have lost it. She felt a little despairing herself. It was always that way—she lost things, or tore them, or got them dirty as no one else in the world seemed to do. Losing her mother's flower at this particular time had the makings of a major catastrophe. What she had to do was hard enough, without having a count like that against her.

"I'm terribly sorry about the flower, Mother. But—but I have to tell you. I'm going to be Mary Evans' associate editor on the *Wand*."

There—she had her mother's startled attention this time. Even the yellow flower was forgotten. Val swallowed lumps of nervousness that seemed to fill her throat and repeated her words. "It's true, Mother. I have to do it."

Mrs. Coleman stared at her in shocked silence for a moment before she found words. "Val, you can't! You mustn't! I know how much it means to you to work on the *Wand* staff, but under circumstances like this—"

"Mother, I'm trying to explain," Val broke in. If only she could find the right words. Clear, sharp words that would state the worst and get it over with. "It's not just because I want to be on the staff that I'm doing this. I think Mary ought to have all the co-operation we can give her. Especially after tonight."

Again Mrs. Coleman made the tired gesture of rubbing her forehead. "Let's not try to discuss this any further just now, Val. I can't help but feel that you're being foolish and impulsive. Perhaps everything will look different to you in a day or two. Then we'll talk about it again. Good-night, dear."

"Good-night, Mother," Val said. Her father looked at her over the top of his book and there was a light in his eyes that said, "Stick by your guns." But he wasn't going to help her. This was her battle and she had to carry it through herself.

She went over and dropped a kiss on his cheek. Then she went upstairs to her room and sat down on her bed.

So she'd done it. But her mother hadn't really believed or understood. The decision had only been pushed ahead. Now she'd have to do it all over again.

What was it Dr. Evans had said tonight? "People working together can split this town into two camps hating each other, bringing misery to all."

Was it going to be like that in her own family? Already there were two camps. She and Nick in one and her mother in another. And that was going to hurt them all. But Dr. Evans had said something else too.

"Or people—all kinds of people working together—can build it into a better town than it's ever been before." Surely that was the true answer, if only her mother would use it.

As she undressed she thought about Mary Evans and the things she had learned about her tonight. Her unexpected talent for dress designing; the fire and spirit that lay behind the quiet mask she wore.

There were two camps in Mary Evans' family, too, with Mary against the kindly ways of her father and the more easy-going Jeff, suspicious of anyone whose skin was white—just as Mrs. Manning was suspicious of anyone whose skin was dark.

Somehow you had to get everybody into *one* camp and get them working together, break down those walls of suspicion and distrust. But how? That was the queston—how?

CHAPTER 11

NICK SETTLES A POINT

Val caught Miss Kay in the corridor the next morning just as she was turning into her office.

"May I speak to you a moment?" she asked. "It's about the *Wand.*"

"Of course, Val. Come in." The principal went ahead and sat down at her desk while Val stood uneasily before her.

"I'm sorry about the way I behaved," she said. "I'd like to be associate editor on the paper if you still want me."

"What made you change your mind, Val?"

"I—I just decided," Val said. "I guess it was the meeting last night. Afterwards, Stephen Reid and I went down to see Mary Evans to tell her."

"I believe your mother is working on one of Mrs. Manning's committee's, isn't she? How does she feel about this?"

"I tried to tell her, but she doesn't understand. I'm going to talk to her again. I want so much to do this, Miss Kay."

There was warm approval in the principal's eyes. "We'll be delighted to have you on the staff. I know this isn't easy for you to do, and I know how disappointed you were not to be editor yourself. I think it's very fair and generous of you to take this stand. We *do* need your help."

The glow of pleasure that went through her was a reward in itself, but there was still difficult details to be settled.

"When must the names of the other staff members be announced?" she asked.

"Mary is working on that now. As soon as she's ready—"

"If I could just have a day or two," Val said. She had to play fair. She had to make sure her mother understood what she was doing before she went ahead.

"I think that can be managed," Miss Kay said. "Mary is coming up to my apartment tonight. Perhaps you could join us. We want to talk over plans and appointments. Bring Judy Piper, if you like. She's a good reporter and Mary wants her on the staff."

"I'd love to come." Val hesitated. "Would it be all right if I brought Stephen Reid, too? He might have some ideas and he's very interested in writing."

Miss Kay nodded approval. "The three of you will be fine. I'm glad you stopped in to see me and that you've changed your mind. Better run now. There's the bell."

Val hurried through the corridor and reached her division room just as the others were sitting down. Tony smiled at her good-naturedly enough, but she had a feeling he was reserving judgment. As he very well might. It hadn't been nice of her to run out on him the night before. But somehow she had felt she would smother if she stayed in that hall another moment. She couldn't have stayed and listened to Tony praise his father. But how was she to make him understand, without hurting his feelings, without making him angry with her?

At least there'd been no trouble at home during breakfast this morning. Her mother had been rested and happy, though a little preoccupied with her committee plans. She was evidently taking it for granted that her daughter would see the light as she wanted her to see it, and Val had mentally postponed the moment of their talk to later in the day. It was still ahead of her and when she thought about it, she could feel the palms of her hands grow moist.

The hours seemed to drag today and she covered herself with no glory in class when she was called on to recite. During lunch period she found a chance to ask Judy and Steve if they'd go with her to Miss Kay's that evening and both agreed. She managed to avoid Tony until the final period was over and she was in the hall closing her locker.

"How come you ran out on me last night?" he asked, leaning against the locker next to hers.

"I'm sorry, Tony," she told him. "Really I am. I know I acted like a drip. But it was so crowded in there and I—I *had* to get outside. "

Tony was not the sort to hold a grudge. He accepted her feeble explanation cheerfully. "Okay. Just so you don't make a habit of it." He turned to his own locker to take out his gym shoes and basketball shorts."

"Practice today?" she asked, eager to drop the other uncomfortable subject.

Tony nodded. "That's right. Nick wants to see what kind of a team he can line up this year. Why don't you and Judy come down to the gym and watch?"

"Maybe we will," Val said.

He was nice. Some boys would have been pretty mad about the way she'd behaved last night. No wonder everyone liked Tony. If only he wasn't on his father's side on the matter of the project.

When he'd gone, Judy took her head out of her own locker and grinned at Val. "The woman's touch," she said, viewing her handiwork with pride.

The interior of Judy's locker was really something, even as high school lockers went. There were pictures of her favorite movie stars, both male and female, pasted all over whatever space there was. The males were the ones she was crazy about at the moment—some eight or ten. The females were the ones she would most like to resemble—a slinky crew, all of them. Hanging from one of the hooks, beneath a raincoat smudgy with pencilled signatures and the blurry outlines of those done optimistically in washable ink, was a crêpe paper vine, complete with bright pink roses. Loot from the senior play last semester. And there was something else.

At the very bottom of the locker, almost hidden by a pile of books and papers, a small printed picture had been pasted in the corner. A picture of Tony Millard that had run in the *Wand* last year. Val turned away quickly so that Judy wouldn't notice that she'd seen it. Tony had been interested in Judy to begin with. Val had not made a play for his attention. How could she help it if he chose to show an interest in Judy's friend?

"Did I hear us get invited to basketball practice?" Judy's voice broke in on her troubled thoughts. "Let's go over to the gym. I sure hope Nick has the makings of a team this year. Come along."

She seemed not to mind the way Tony had asked them through Val, or that Val had gone out with him the night before. But the glimpse of that picture in her friend's locker continued to trouble Val.

A handful of girls had dropped into the gallery above the

gym floor to watch. Judy and Val found seats down near the front, where they could lean against the rail and look over at the rectangle of floor below.

"My goodness!" Judy whispered. "Will you look at that Jeff Evans!"

The Negro boy, thinner and lankier than ever in basketball shorts, was handling the ball with a touch that showed he loved it. The long-fingered hands that had held a hurt pup's paw so gently the day before, knew how to coax a response out of leather too. That ball was doing things it wouldn't do even for Tony Millard.

Over against the windows Nick stood with his whistle in hand, watching intently. He looked quick and alert, ready to control any situation which might arise. His eyes followed Jeff with keen interest as the boy took the ball down the floor in a long dribble, without looking at it once, and then wheeled to drop an amazingly accurate basket shot.

"There's Tony," Judy said. "What's the matter with him?"

Tony, too, was watching Jeff. He was seated on a dusty pile of canvas pads tying his shoes, but his eyes didn't miss a move Jeff made and there was a struggle of some kind going on in him.

"It's beginning to happen," Val whispered.

"What's beginning to happen? What are you talking about?"

Val hunted for words to express the thought which had struck her. "I was thinking about it last night at the meeting, Judy. I mean the way Tony is as crazy about basketball as he is about his father."

"So what?" Judy regarded her blankly.

"Don't you see? Jeff Evans looks like the best prospect

Willow High has ever seen when it comes to basketball.
Tony can't help recognizing that. But Tony's father is down
on Negroes, so Tony probably feels Jeff hasn't any business
being as good as he is. He's being pulled in two directions.
I hope basketball wins."

"It had better win," Judy whispered back. "Or since
Tony's captain of the team, there'll be trouble."

Jeff made another spectacular basket and Judy burst into
impulsive applause. Val nudged her into silence.

"Nick'll throw you out. He won't have applause at
practice."

"I know." Judy subsided shamefacedly. "But did you ever
in your life see anything like it?"

Nick had looked up and scowled, but now his attention
turned back to that long-legged boy on the floor, with the
big hands that could hold a basketball in a way Val had
never seen one held before. A few reproving glances had
turned Judy's way and then shifted back to the floor, but
there was something odd about the watchers, both in the
balcony and among the boys grouped below.

If Tony Millard had been out there putting on a perform-
ance like this, the watchers would have been unable to
contain themselves. Now there was a tenseness in their fixed
gaze, almost as if they were seeing something they didn't
want to see.

Had that meeting last night started its poison seeping
through the town already, Val wondered unhappily?

Nick reached out and stopped the ball as it went by. His
words reached the balcony crowd clearly and Val knew he
meant everyone in the room to hear them.

"If you can work with a team as well as you can handle a

ball, we can use you, Jeff," he said. "But there's more to playing basketball than making baskets." He turned from the
eager smile on the Negro boy's face and looked across the
floor at the others. "Well? What are you waiting for? How
about getting in on this? The kid here doesn't own the ball."

Stephen Reid came out on the floor and Nick tossed the
ball to him. Val leaned over the rail to see better. Steve
looked slight beside the big fellows, but there was a natural
grace to his movements and he quite evidently had speed. He
and Jeff were running down the floor now, with the ball
moving between them in sure, quick arcs.

Nobody else had moved. Tony's head was down as he bent
over his shoes. Nick blew his whistle and the play stopped.

"Out on the floor!" he snapped.

They came as if they couldn't make up their minds about
something. Most of the boys were looking uncertainly at
Tony, waiting for him to speak. He came out more slowly
than the others.

"Look, Nick," he said, "Jeff's pretty good with a basketball.
We can all see that. But he doesn't belong on this team."

"Say what you mean!" Nick snapped.

Tony looked thoroughly uncomfortable, but he went on.
"I guess we'd just as soon not have a black boy on this team,
Nick. There are others of them coming up here—why don't
they start a team of their own and—"

The thud and bounce of a ball striking the floor cut him
short. The smile of pride and eagerness had been wiped off
Jeff's face. He had thrown the ball down violently and was
stalking off toward the dressing rooms. Nick's bark followed
him.

"Nobody's been dismissed. Back on the floor, Jeff! Line up, all of you!"

Val could feel Judy's hand tight on her arm, responding to the tension of the moment. If they didn't obey—if they went into open rebellion—

But Jeff had turned and was coming reluctantly back across the floor to stand next to Steve. The quick anger had gone out of him, but so had his eager, cheerful air. He looked a little like Mary now; like someone who had been hurt and had put up his guard so as not to be hurt again.

After a second or two the others lined up, leaving Jeff at one end. Nick stepped out to the middle of the floor and looked them over as if he did not like what he saw.

"Maybe we'd better get a few things straight right now," he said. "As long as I'm coach here I'm running this team. If any of you don't like how it's run you can drop out. And you better do it now because I don't want any dead wood getting in the way later on. You fellows didn't make such a hot showing last year. This year there's going to be no soft stuff. Willow High's going to have a *team*.

"If you want to stay on it, Tony, there'll be no more talk like that. Basketball—*winning* basketball means teamwork. That goes for you, too, Jeff. Flashy play's no good unless it fits in. And if anybody else walks off the floor before I say he can, I'll suspend him. That clear?"

Nobody said a word. When Nick began assigning positions, they moved out on the floor and a practice game started. It was routine stuff now. The rebellion had been squelched.

Val felt limp and at the same time terribly proud. Nick had what it took. She was glad that Steve had seen him like that—living up to what Steve's father had said about him.

Maybe Willow High *could* have a team this year. And maybe with a player on their side like Jeff Evans showed promise of being, they'd make a showing for a change. Maybe even land near the top. And then there wouldn't be any more talk about Nick Coleman not being such a hot coach.

Her own lagging courage had been helped by what she had just seen and she sat up straight in her seat.

"I'm going home, Judy. There's something I have to do. I'll see you tonight."

There was something she had to do all right. Something she had to stand up to just as Nick had stood up to what might have been a serious outbreak on the gym floor. She had to go home and talk straight out to her mother. Just as straight as Nick had talked to those kids. When she got through this time there mustn't be any doubt in her mother's mind about where she stood or what she meant to do.

CHAPTER 12

"LET'S DO SOMETHING!"

Mrs. Coleman was on the rear terrace arranging flowers in a vase. Her neat green cotton frock was creaseless and the roll of hair away from her forehead showed no blowing strands. Today the frown of worry was gone and she looked happy and contented and young as her quick hands moved among the flowers.

Val wished she could let her stay like that and not bring back that worried frown. If only there were some gentle way to do this. But there was no way except to go through with it as quickly as possible.

"Mother," she said, "I have to tell you. I have to make you see. I don't want the post of associate on the *Wand* just to be on the staff. I want to help Mary Evans."

Mrs. Coleman set the flowers down. "Val, honey, I know you want to be nice, but in a case like this you mustn't let your kindness of heart run away with you."

"But, Mother, we *do* say all that about liberty-and-justice —you said it yourself at the meeting. So why—?"

"When you're older you'll understand, Val. All this is terribly complex. I'm not sure I understand all the angles myself. But there are people in this town who do understand and I feel that we ought to let them—"

"Think for us?" Val cried. "But why? Maybe I don't understand all this yet. But I—I have a feeling about it. And I *want* to understand."

"Of course, dear. But while you're trying you mustn't do anything as foolish as this. What do you think Mrs. Manning will say if she hears that I allowed my daughter to work with a Negro girl on the *Wand?*"

Val wanted to say that she didn't care what Mrs. Manning thought, but her mother looked so thoroughly unhappy that she didn't have the heart to speak the thought.

Mrs. Coleman had picked up a spray of flowers and she spoke without looking up. "Are you really going through with this, Val?"

If her mother had commanded, used authority, she might have rebelled, but against her gentleness she had no weapon. She wanted to go over and put her arms about her, plead with her not to listen to Mrs. Manning, to try to see the other side. But she knew it wouldn't be any use. There was only one choice left.

"I have to go through with it," she said. "But if it will make you feel better I won't take an official post. I'll keep my name out of it."

Her mother brightened a little. "I'd appreciate that, dear. I'm sure it will be the wiser way."

She put the last of the flowers into the vase and carried it into the kitchen. Val stood by the table, picking up bits of stems, breaking them into tiny pieces. Apparently her mother did not believe there was much she could do toward helping Mary. It was more the idea of having her daughter's name attached to the title of associate editor that had mattered to Mrs. Coleman.

Perhaps her mother was right and there was nothing the weaker camp could do against the strength of the Manning-Millard group. But she didn't want to believe that yet. There must be some way. Perhaps Miss Kay would have some ideas on the subject tonight. She could still attend the meeting, even though she would have to withdraw her offer to be associate editor before she'd even had a chance at the job.

At dinner she was uneasy for fear the things which had happened at basketball practice that afternoon would come up for discussion, but no one said anything. As if by agreement Steve and Nick stuck to safe subjects.

Later, when the dishes were done, Judy came over to go with her to the meeting and while they were waiting till it was time to leave, they cornered Nick and Steve on the terrace, out of Mrs. Coleman's hearing.

"How did the rest of the practice go?" Val demanded. "Was there any more trouble?"

Nick shook his head. "Tony didn't like it much, but that's too bad. They all loosened up after they got going."

"Looks like good stuff for a team," Steve said.

"It'll be okay. What Tony and Jeff need is to get to know each other. Maybe that's always the answer—getting to know people."

Steve looked interested. "That gives me an idea."

"What?" asked Judy the curious.

"Something I saw done in a department store where I worked last summer. It might work here. But I'd like to think about it for a while before I go springing it half-cocked. Maybe I can ask Miss Kay about it tonight."

"Mm," said Judy. "Maybe that gives me an idea, too. Nick,

do you really think that's the answer—getting people to know each other?"

"It's part of it. Getting 'em to work together until the first thing you know they aren't suspicious any more."

Judy jumped from her perch on the arm of Val's chair. "Look, kids, you go ahead to Miss Kay's. I have an assignment I've just given myself. I'll be along later."

Val regarded her friend uneasily. She had cause to know that Judy's inspirations did not always turn out for the best.

"Maybe you'd better tell us what you're up to first," she said.

Judy's eyes danced with a dangerous light. "I've just had a brilliant idea. Grown-ups are hopeless—you can't do anything with 'em. But you *can* do something with people our age. There's somebody I want to bring to that meeting tonight. Don't worry. I'll manage."

And off she went, every red hair bouncing with eagerness.

Val sighed. "Goodness knows what will happen now. When Judy has inspirations things start popping. Well, there's no stopping her. Suppose we get going, Steve."

The walk across town was a quiet one. Val was busy wondering what Judy might be up to, who on earth she meant to bring to the meeting. If only she'd phone Miss Kay and ask her about it first. But asking permission wasn't a strong point with Judy. Steve, too, was busy with his own thoughts. Probably about this department store scheme he had mentioned. At any rate, they did little talking.

When they were a block away from the big apartment building where Miss Kay lived, a tall slim girl turned in from a side street and walked quickly ahead of them.

"Mary!" Val called. "Wait for us!"

Mary Evans looked around and slowed her steps until Val and Steve reached her side.

"Your brother Jeff's a whizz at basketball," Val told her as the three went on together. "He's going to do a lot for the team."

"If they let him play," Mary said.

"Of course they'll let him play. My father wants him on the team and he told them all what was what today in the gym. Didn't he, Steve?"

"He sure did." Steve backed her up. "And Val's right about Jeff being good. Tony had to see that."

"What about Tony's father?" Mary asked.

Val didn't know the answer to that. In fact, she hadn't thought about it till this minute. Mr. Millard certainly wouldn't approve when he heard that Jeff Evans was being given a chance on the team. The question was what he might do because of his disapproval.

They walked on in silence until they reached the building where Miss Kay lived with a married sister. It was owned by the Millard Real Estate Company and housed some of the town's best apartments.

When they entered the lobby Mary moved away from them.

"Where are you going?" Val called after her. "The elevator is this way."

"Don't wait for me," Mary said quietly. "I'll meet you upstairs."

Steve understood first. "Maybe there's a rule in the building, Val," he said in a low voice. "I mean—about using the front elevator."

Behind them the car door had opened and Val turned to

watch a befurred woman with a Pekinese in her arms step into it.

"You mean they'll let a—a—pooch like that go up in the car and won't take Mary?" Val asked indignantly.

Steve settled the matter quickly. "We can't do anything about the rules, but if we don't care for the company in the front elevator, we don't have to take it. Let's go around and go up with Mary."

That suited Val and they hurried to the rear of the building and reached the self-service freight elevator just as Mary stepped into it.

"We're coming this way, too," Val said.

Mary accepted their presence without comment, but her guard was up and Val felt a little sick with hurt for her.

There were no soft lights, polished wood panels, or thick carpeting on the floor of this car, but Steve looked about him with approval.

"I like this better," he said. "It's more my speed."

In spite of his valiant effort, they rode up in an embarrassed silence. There wasn't anything they could say to make a thing like this less hurtful.

Miss Kay welcomed them cheerfully into a bright, attractive living room.

"Where is Judy?" she asked as they settled into chairs. "We can't start without that live wire."

"Then you haven't heard from her?" Val said. "I was hoping she might call you, but I suppose that was asking too much. She's had one of her inspirations and I don't know what she's up to. I'm expecting the worst. She said there was someone she wanted to bring to the meeting."

Miss Kay smiled. "No use worrying about it. We'll find

out what she's up to in due time. Val, have you decided
whether you can take the post of associate editor on the
Wand?"

This was going to be hard to do. Val threw a quick look at
Mary and then faced Miss Kay.

"I'm sorry, but I can't take it as far as the name goes. But
I wonder if you'd let me help any way I can without being
officially on the staff?"

Mary wouldn't need any pictures drawn. She would understand without explanation that Val's mother had objected.

Miss Kay understood, too. "Thank you for your offer,
Val," she said gently. "I know Mary and I will be grateful
for any help you can give us. This year our problem isn't
just a matter of turning out a good paper. We'll need to use
the *Wand* to help prove to the community that inside the
school we can work our new problems out in a constructive,
democratic way."

"You mean through articles?" Val asked.

"Yes, and news items. It might be interesting to work out
a study of all the races that have made up the people of this
town. If we go back only a little way, we are all foreigners,
you know. What do you think about trying that?"

"I think it would be fine," Val said. "Don't you, Mary?"

The other girl shrugged. "Maybe. I don't think it will do
much good. We need more than words."

Steve turned away from the window and the others looked
at him. He spoke a little hesitantly.

"I know I'm new at Willow High and I don't want to talk
out of turn, but I've been thinking about something Nick
Coleman said this evening. He said it was all in people getting to know each other."

Miss Kay gave him her interested attention. "We'd like to hear any suggestions you care to make, Stephen."

"This hasn't anything to do with the *Wand*," Steve went on. "But it seems to me that it's like Mary says. We have to do more toward getting to know each other than just studying about racial heritages and stuff like that. I don't mean that isn't important. It sounds like a swell idea. But I've been thinking about last summer when I clerked for a while in a department store in San Francisco."

"Let's hear about it, Stephen," Miss Kay said.

"Well, they had a system there for breaking in new clerks. They had older clerks in every department they called 'angels.' When a new clerk came in he was assigned to an angel who looked after him. You know—answered questions, and steered him right, got him out of tangles, gave him advice. The angels used to get pretty interested in seeing their charges make good."

"That sounds like a good system," Miss Kay said.

"What I was wondering was why it couldn't be applied just as well in a school."

"Steve, that's super!" Val broke in. "You mean have every new student assigned to an older student who'd play angel and look after him? Let's do it!"

Miss Kay looked at Mary Evans. "What do you think, Mary?"

"You mean to have certain white students look after Negro students?" Mary asked.

"Yes," Miss Kay said. "We'd like to know what you think."

Mary shook her head dubiously. "I don't think it would work. I don't think the white students would want to do it."

"Of course we would!" Val cried. "Anyway, I would. And I'm sure Judy would."

"I don't think Tony Millard or Dorothy Manning would care much about the idea," Mary said.

"It wouldn't be compulsory," Steve added. "That would defeat the whole thing. But you could give it a build-up and then call for volunteers. Nobody would have to help who didn't want to."

"Stephen," Miss Kay said warmly, "I believe you've hit on a real idea. If it works it will give the new students a feeling that we want to welcome them and help them to fit in. And it will be an awfully good way of getting our older students interested in the newcomers."

"If it works," Mary said. "I don't think it will."

Miss Kay shook her head. "We can't be defeatists."

"It isn't that." Mary's slim brown hands made a gesture of protest. "It's just that I know what to expect. I wish it would work, but I don't think it will."

"Let's *make* it work," Val said. "No failures allowed."

Before they could continue the discussion, Miss Kay's doorbell rang and she crossed the room to the little hallway.

"Hold your breath everybody," Val said. "Here comes Judy with her bombshell."

From where she sat Val could not see into the hall, but she could hear Judy's lively tones and then the softer tones of another girl. Tones that made her wince in recognition. A glance at Mary told her that she had recognized the newcomer's voice, too, and was retreating more deeply than ever into her protective shell.

How could anybody as bright as Judy do such a crazy

thing? Val thought helplessly. And without asking for a word of advice from anybody.

Judy strutted gayly into the room. If she held a bomb with a lighted fuse in her cute little hands, she was apparently oblivious of the fact. Miss Kay followed her, with Dorothy Manning at her side. The expression on the principal's face might do for a copy of the Sphinx, Val thought. Inscrutable —that's what it was.

"You see," Judy bubbled happily, "since this meeting is to make plans for the *Wand,* I thought Dorothy ought to be here."

What connection pretty Dorothy Manning, who went in for no school activities unless they had to do with dances and parties, might have with the *Wand* was a mystery to everybody, so Judy's announcement met with silence.

Judy was undismayed. "We need more social stuff in the *Wand.* You know—nice gossipy paragraphs about who's running around with which, and party reporting, and style and beauty notes."

"That sounds interesting," Miss Kay said quietly. "But I didn't know you cared much about writing, Dorothy."

Dorothy opened her mouth, but Judy gave her no chance to answer. "Oh, she doesn't. But she knows all that stuff better than anybody else in school. So I figured she could tell it to me and I could sort of—ghostwrite it."

"That's a possibility," Miss Kay said. "Of course we'll have to consult our editor about it. Find yourselves places, girls."

Dorothy crossed the room to drape herself gracefully into a chair with a high tapestry back that framed her like a picture.

She saw Mary for the first time as she dropped into the

chair, and Val saw the look of delicate shock that went over
her face. At school Mary was someone she could easily ignore.
Probably she forgot most of the time that the Negro girl was
in the same room with her. But here in Miss Kay's apartment, Mary Evans was definitely one of the group and could
not be overlooked.

Miss Kay spoke quietly. "We're glad to have you here,
Dorothy. This is a planning meeting. One of the plans we've
been discussing has to do with an idea Stephen Reid has
suggested. Suppose you tell Judy and Dorothy about it,
Stephen."

While Steve went over his angel plan again, Val took the
opportunity to give Judy a look that was as disapproving as
she could make it. But Judy merely beamed in response and
continued to look pleased with herself.

Steve's plan clicked with Judy at once and she said so in
no uncertain terms. "That's wonderful. And it will really do
what your father was talking about tonight, Val—get people
to know each other. That's why I brought Dorothy here tonight—so she could have a better chance to get acquainted
with Mary."

That statement was met by a moment of dead silence and
then Miss Kay began to talk about editorial plans for the
Wand. Dorothy's cheeks were pink and Val could suspect the
story she would take home to her mother. But at least she
kept her thoughts to herself for the moment. Mary behaved
with her usual quiet reserve and revealed no emotion of
any kind.

Before the many discussions had come to an end, Dorothy
announced that she had to go home. She left with a parting
shot.

"Of course I'd love to help Judy with party news and school gossip—after the editorial staff gets straightened out."

Miss Kay walked with her to the door. "What do you mean by that, Dorothy?"

Her answer came back to them clearly. "Lots of us think Val Coleman should have been editor. Mother does. She's taking it up with the school board."

"The school board," Miss Kay said firmly, "is not the committee which appoints the *Wand* editor. That is a post which is awarded for merit and hard work. There will be no change."

The door closed after Dorothy and Miss Kay came back to the room with a curious mixture of dismay and amusement on her face.

"This is one of the times when a sense of humor is more important than anything else," she said. "We mustn't let this upset us. There's no use being hurt or indignant or angry. We might just as well sit down and laugh."

"At what?" Judy demanded.

"At you, darling," Val said weakly. "For thinking that the way to get people to understand each other is to fling them violently at each other's heads."

"But I thought if Dorothy could be made to want to get her name in the *Wand*, she'd be willing to—to—" Judy's words faded off without ending the sentence. "Maybe I didn't think it through," she said. "Maybe I did jump without looking where I was jumping. Mary, I'm terribly sorry. Honestly, I *thought* it was a good idea."

There was no doubting Judy's sincerity or her good intentions. To the relief of everyone Mary smiled. Perhaps it

wasn't outright laughter, perhaps it wasn't too steady a smile
—but she had the courage to manage it.

"This reminds me of a Bill Mauldin cartoon I saw a while
ago," she said. "Two children were walking down a street
and one child was telling the other that she couldn't play
with him because her mother said he had 'minorities.' I'm
afraid that's the disease Dorothy Manning thinks I have and
she can't play with me."

They all laughed a little shakily and Judy said "Women's
clubs!" in as scornful a tone as she could manage.

Miss Kay shook her head. "Wait a minute. Women's clubs
do a great deal of good in this country and they wield a lot of
power. Many of them are working right now for the cause of
racial understanding. It's unfortunate that here in Willow
Hill the wrong kind of leadership has taken over."

Shortly after that, the meeting broke up.

"We're only six flights up," Val said as they left Miss Kay's
apartment, "and I feel like doing something violent. Let's
walk down."

She managed a whispered explanation of the elevator situation to Judy and they all trooped down six flights of stairs
in not too quiet fashion. At the third floor they passed the
up-coming elevator and when the door opened to let someone out, Val had to suppress Judy with a pinch to keep her
from making a face at the car full of people.

A block from the building Mary left them to turn toward
her own home and Val, Judy and Steve walked on together.

"I keep thinking about what Dr. Evans said the other
night," Val said. "I mean about all kinds of people working
together to make this a better town. I wish we could get

some of the people together who aren't on the side of the Mannings and the Millards."

Judy shook her head. "I think the only way to do it is to work through the kids. It's just like I said—grown-ups are hopeless. Look at my mother. She doesn't mind the project a bit. But she's busy. She doesn't want to be bothered. And dad's tired when he comes home at night. He wants to take his shoes off and have a nap. He says he has troubles enough of his own without worrying about the Rights of Man."

"I wish we could find somebody," Val said. "Somebody really important in this town—who'd be willing to stand up against Mr. Millard and start something for the other side."

"It would be worth a try," Steve agreed. "So far Tony's father thinks public opinion is all on his side."

"Well, it's not!" Val said. But she didn't feel nearly so confident as she sounded.

CHAPTER 13

ANGELS

The next morning Val caught Nick just as he was leaving the house. "Any objections to your daughter tagging along?" she asked. "Or do you prefer your own thoughts?"

He smiled as she slipped her hand through his arm and she knew he was glad to have her company.

"I'm awfully glad you settled things by putting Jeff on the team," she told him. "Do you think there'll be trouble?"

"Maybe. Things are okay right now. It all depends."

"Do you think Tony will behave?"

"There's no telling. Trouble is, he gets a slant at home that makes it tough for him to fit in when Jeff Evans is playing."

"Is there any way his father could make trouble for you? I mean about putting Jeff on the team?"

Nick did not answer right away and his silence was disturbing. Then he patted her hand where it rested on his arm.

"Don't let's cross bridges. Maybe he could, but maybe he won't think it's important enough to try."

"If you could just whip together a good enough team before he catches on!" Val cried. "I mean if Willow High could

come up with a team that started toward the top—with Jeff
Evans on it—you'd have an argument nobody could beat."

There was a twinkle in Nick's eyes. "That's the general
idea I'm working on. It won't be easy, but if I can get those
kids to forget personal grudges and work together, there's
real stuff there this year."

"You *can* do it!" Val put all the assurance she was capable
of into her words. "And I don't see how Tony could resist
the idea of a winning team."

They were getting near school and she hadn't broached
the matter she'd wanted to ask him about. She went on
quickly.

"That meeting the other night—I don't think all the people there were haters. There must have been some who
didn't feel like Mr. Millard."

"I expect you're right," Nick said.

"But the trouble is those people aren't doing anything. If
we could just get them interested enough to want to help the
Negroes, instead of trying to throw them out—"

"That's a big hunk you're biting off," Nick told her. "But
go ahead. I'm all for you. Where you going to start?"

"That's it. Where can we start? Do you know anybody I
could go to see? Somebody who'd be really important in this
town and who might listen?"

Nick had no immediate answer. "Suppose you give me
time to think that over. I'll see what I can figure out and
let you know later. Okay?"

Now that she had a plan in mind she wanted to get to
work on it that very instant. But there was no choice at the
moment except to wait. So she told him "okay" and ran
ahead to catch Judy as she was going up the school steps.

As they walked through the corridors together, Val noted that the new Negro students were really in evidence now. They stood in groups all through the halls, always together, not mingling with the others.

"I wonder how soon Miss Kay will get this angel business started?" Judy said, and unexpectedly had her answer at once.

There was a crowd around the big bulletin board near the stairs and Val and Judy pushed in to see what was attracting attention. Miss Kay must have drawn up the notice after they'd left her apartment last night. It was not typed, the way official notices usually were, but boldly lettered poster fashion in India ink. Val and Judy stood beside the others reading.

DO YOU WANT TO BE AN "ANGEL?"

WE MEAN AN "ANGEL" OF THE EARTHLY VARIETY—A SPONSOR.
OUR "ANGELS" WILL SPONSOR NEW STUDENTS.
THEY WILL HELP THEM TO FIND FRIENDS
AND FIT INTO SCHOOL LIFE.
THIS MORNING TEACHERS WILL CALL FOR VOLUNTEERS.
IF YOU WANT TO BE AN "ANGEL," LET US KNOW.

The constantly changing group around the bulletin board was abuzz. Few of the Negro students approached the board, but evidently its message had reached them, for they were whispering animatedly among themselves all through the corridors. Reaction among the white students was apparently varied. Val heard a few scoffing remarks, but for the most part there was an attitude of waiting and wanting to hear more about it.

When they reached the upper corridor Tony was at his locker.

"Hi, gals," he said as they came up. "How do you like my sprouting wings?"

Val and Judy exchanged startled looks.

"Don't tell us *you're* going to be an angel!" Judy cried.

Tony laughed good-naturedly. "Why not? Miss Kay is calling for volunteer lunatics, isn't she? Why won't I do?"

"Oh, Tony!" Judy wailed. "This is serious. It isn't a joke. We've got to help these new students fit in so there won't be trouble inside the school."

"There'll be trouble," Tony said confidently. "Dad gives us just about a month before there's a blowup. You can't do anything to stop it. Maybe the sooner it comes the better for all of us. Maybe this angel business will help it along. Dad says the Negroes ought to have their own school."

Because it was Tony Val wanted to stay out of it. On everything but this one point she liked him so much. If he could just be changed around on this! But his words stung her to answer.

"That's Jim Crow, Tony," she told him. "We don't believe in that in the north."

"Who says we don't? And it's the way it ought to be, too."

"What about basketball?" Val asked. She couldn't resist that.

"There, too," he said quickly. "I tried to tell Nick they ought to have their own team."

"Nick thinks we need Jeff pretty badly," Val said. "With you and Steve and Jeff maybe we'll have a winning combination."

Tony wasn't very good at concealing his feelings. For just

an instant the struggle between loyalty to his father and desire to see Willow High come out on top with a winning
basketball team was plain for anyone to see.

Judy saw the drift and came quickly to Val's aid. "Oh,
Tony, wouldn't it be swell to have a winning team?"

"Cut it out, you two," Tony said. "It isn't going to work.
You can't count on those people. You'll see. Even if this Jeffy
boy looks pretty good, he'll fall down when it comes to the
clinch. They always do."

Judy's red hair seemed to grow redder as she listened. "I
know—'dad says.' Don't you ever think for yourself, Tony
Millard?"

Judy stood before him with her hands jauntily on her hips
and her chin in the air, while Tony glowered down at her.
Then, unexpectedly, he laughed.

"Okay, squirt. Maybe I am thinking for myself. Maybe
that's why I'm going to volunteer for this angel business.
Maybe this will give me a chance—"

He stopped abruptly and Val looked around for the cause
of the interruption. Miss Kay was just going into the division
room to speak to Mrs. Harcourt. If she had heard Tony's
words, she gave no sign.

"I hope she heard you!" Judy stormed. "If you're not sincere she won't let you be a sponsor."

Tony recovered himself. "She's calling for volunteers, isn't
she? It will look pretty funny if she turns me down."

"And I suppose you're going to take on one of these new
kids and make his life miserable," Judy said. "I think you're
an absolute heel, Tony Millard."

"No you don't." He was laughing at her openly. "Sometimes you even like me. I'm not going to make anybody's life miserable, but I'd like to show these Negroes that they can't fit in. If they get that idea, they'll want to be out of this school in a hurry."

Judy turned away and slammed her locker door furiously shut.

"It's a good thing you're not wearing a hat," Tony said. "It would go up in flames. Bet that hair of yours is sizzling right now."

He moistened a finger and reached it toward her, but Judy flounced out of reach and went into Mrs. Harcourt's room. Miss Kay came out at that moment and Val looked after her thoughtfully. What Tony intended to do might have serious consequences. But if they turned him down as a volunteer, that might have serious consequences too. She left Tony still laughing over Judy's fiery temper and flew down the corridor after Miss Kay.

The principal turned as she reached her side and Val rushed breathlessly into words.

"Miss Kay, did you hear what Tony's going to do?"

Miss Kay nodded. "Yes, I heard. And I can imagine his purpose."

"If he gets away with it he could spoil the whole plan," Val said. "Some of the others might follow his lead and it would be worse than if we didn't try it at all."

"I know," Miss Kay nodded worriedly. "There's a way out. Stephen Reid is a new student. We could assign him to Tony and that might close the whole matter."

Val considered that doubtfully. Of course Steve would have to have a sponsor, too. They couldn't make it pointedly just the Negro students.

"I'm afraid Tony will make something of it if you work

it that way," she said. "I—I've a sort of crazy idea. Maybe it isn't any good. But it might be a way to put the scheme across and tie Tony's hands."

Miss Kay listened as she poured out the plan that had come to her and after a moment the principal's face lighted.

"Val, I believe you've hit it. It's just possible this might work. I'll go back and see what Mrs. Harcourt thinks."

She hurried back to the division room and Val returned to her locker with her heart pounding against her ribs. Now that the die was cast, the thing she had suggested was beginning to frighten her. If it failed it might do an awful lot of damage.

Tony was waiting for her and he had stopped laughing. "You, too?" he said. "Women! You can't trust 'em."

Val got her books out of her locker without answering and went past him into the room just as the bell rang. She glanced at Steve as she sat down, wondering what he would think of what she had done, wishing she had had time to ask him about it before she flew into action. But it was too late for wishing now. And Miss Kay seemed to think it was a chance worth taking.

When they'd settled down to quiet Mrs. Harcourt picked up a paper from her desk.

"I suppose most of you have seen the bulletin on the board downstairs," she said. "I want to explain it a bit more fully before I call for volunteer angels.

"With so many new students coming into Willow High there is going to be a great deal of confusion unless all of us work together to lessen it. This isn't like a group of freshmen coming in. They can be handled in one body. But these people are going into various classes and rooms and they need help."

The room was quiet and attentive, but Val sensed again that queer tension she had felt in the auditorium. It wasn't anything you could put your finger on. It hadn't really come into the open as it had among their elders at the rally, but it was here among the young people too. If it wasn't dispelled, there would certainly be trouble.

"Miss Kay has made an excellent suggestion," Mrs. Harcourt continued. "Just as some department stores use sponsors to look after new clerks, we are going to have such sponsors here. We like the department store nickname of 'angel' and we're going to use that, too."

Val looked around and caught Steve's eye and smiled. Somehow, she was proud that it was his idea. Then she turned back to follow Mrs. Harcourt's words.

"Of course these angels must be responsible people. They must be sincerely helpful and they must be on their toes to assist in every way they can. It will be the duty of each angel to see that his particular ward fits comfortably and constructively into our school life. It will, of course, be a reflection upon the angel if he fails."

That was good, Val thought. Perhaps it would make Tony less willing to volunteer.

"Now then," Mrs. Harcourt said, "I'd like volunteers, please. Girls will sponsor girls and boys will sponsor boys. Hands, please."

Val and Judy put up their hands at once and other hands went up around the room. Out of the corner of her eye Val could see Tony start to put his hand up, then pull it down. She was almost ready to breathe more easily when Judy turned her red head and gave him a scornful look. That was the worst thing she could have done. Tony grinned at her and waved his hand energetically.

Quietly Mrs. Harcourt wrote down the names, calling them aloud as she did so. She called Tony's name last and he pulled down his hand with an air of satisfaction. Next came the assigning.

"Judy, you may take Ella Tucker. Ella, put up your hand so that Judy can see who you are."

A girl in the second row raised her hand and looked around at Judy. She was a little thing with a big sunny smile and a sparkle in her dark eyes. She looked friendly and as if she might be fun.

"Val, you may take Lavina Dixon."

The girl named Lavina had to be prodded to put up her hand and she did not turn her head to look at Val.

Oh, dear, Val thought. It *would* be her luck to get somebody who didn't want to be friendly.

It was gratifying that there were more volunteers than there were Negro students in the room, so a few outside assignments had to be made. Mrs. Harcourt ran quickly down the list, until even Steve had been assigned to another boy in the room and everyone had been called except Tony. Val held her breath. This was it—win or lose.

"I'm not too sure about your qualifications in the matter of responsibility, Tony," the teacher said. "I seem to recall hearing about a few low marks last semester. However, we are willing to give you a try. You may sponsor Jeff Evans who is in Room 10."

Judy twisted in her seat to look at Val, dismay in her eyes, and Val felt her hope sinking. Tony looked altogether too pleased. He was cocking an eyebrow triumphantly at them both. Once more Val's eyes sought Steve's across the room and he nodded at her. He didn't know, of course, that she was back of this assignment, but he had caught the possible implications quickly.

That was it, of course. That was why Tony looked so pleased. He hadn't been as quick as Steve to see what he might be up against. It would be one thing to take on some boy who didn't play basketball and set to work undermining his courage, making him feel unwelcome in the school. But it would be something else to do that to Jeff Evans, because to succeed at it might mean ruining the outlook of the team. By putting Jeff in Tony's charge, it was just possible they might clip Tony's wings.

Mrs. Harcourt had more to say. "Your duties, angels, will start at once. Get on the job as soon as possible and be helpful in every way you can. It isn't just a matter of assisting about classes and general study problems. It is a matter of helping your wards to fit into school life. Find out what their interests are and what can be done to develop those interests. See if you can really earn the title of 'angel.' I suggest that you come back to this room during lunch period today and have a talk with the person you've been assigned to help."

The bell for first period rang and they broke up to go to classes. Ella Tucker waited for Judy by the door and Val heard her words as she went by.

"Gosh!" Ella was saying, "I sure do need an angel. I'm all mixed up. Do you think—"

Judy was going to do all right. She'd take over the management of Ella's problems in a way that would probably end up in a grand muddle, with both of them in need of angels.

But they'd end up friends. Val turned to look for her own
charge, but Lavina Dixon had not waited to speak to her.
She caught a last glimpse of the girl as she turned a corner
in the corridor without a backward glance.

Someone else stopped beside her and Val looked around
at Mary Evans. She had forgotten about Mary in her worry
over what Tony meant to do. She had not stopped to consider what Mary's reaction might be in this matter. There
was cold anger in the other girl's eyes, but she spoke in a
tone so low that only Val could hear.

"You see what this foolish angel business is going to do?
I don't see how Miss Kay could be so unkind as to put Tony
Millard in charge of Jeff!"

"That was my idea," Val confessed. "And it certainly isn't
meant as an unkindness. Don't you see, Mary—"

But Mary would not wait for her explanation. She went
on quickly and her voice trembled a little with the depth of
her feeling.

"I see all right. Do you think Tony's going to be decent
and helpful to Jeff? Of course he isn't. He's going to hurt
him. And Jeff won't know how to defend himself because he
can't understand cruelty. Jeff's kind and—and *good*. He
thinks other people are just like he is. He trusts everybody.
He'll trust Tony, too, and what Tony will do to him—"

She turned abruptly away and walked down the corridor
alone. Val was torn between her own rising indignation and
a desire to run after Mary and try to explain the side to this
she hadn't seen. Indignation won out.

Mary was impossible. It was just as she had thought in the
beginning—you couldn't help someone who didn't want your
help. Well, she wasn't going to offer her friendship again.

Let Mary think what she chose. No one knew what the outcome would be, or who was right. She could just be glad that Mary wasn't her problem. Even that sullen looking girl, Lavina Dixon, would be easier to deal with than Mary.

However, she was not so sure of this later in the morning when she and Judy finished lunch and went upstairs to find Ella and Lavina waiting for them, along with others who had been turned over to angels. Jeff wasn't there, so evidently Tony had had to go to his room to talk to him.

Val dropped into a seat in front of Lavina and tried to think of something cheerful and friendly to say. The other girl glanced at her and then off into space. She was rather an attractive girl, but she seemed to be occupying a wedge of space that had no room in it for Val Coleman.

Across the room Val could hear Judy chattering away to Ella Tucker. There was no trouble there, she thought enviously. Find out the interest of the new students, Mrs. Harcourt had said. But how did you go about it when you couldn't get a word out of someone?

"Do you like basketball?" Val ventured.

The girl shook her head.

"That's too bad," Val went on, "because I think we're going to have a pretty good team this year and we're hoping the whole school will get interested enough to back up the team."

What Lavina Dixon thought about that was a mystery. Val remembered some advice Nick had given her once when she'd been angry with someone. "Put yourself in the other fellow's shoes," he'd said. "If you can feel how he feels, maybe you won't be so mad at him."

She shut her eyes for a moment and tried to imagine how

Lavina must feel coming to a new school where she might not be wanted. Why on earth should she care whether or not they had a basketball team? But in this case there was a reason for her to care.

"Do you know Jeff Evans?" Val asked.

The girl looked at her directly for the first time. "Sure, I know Jeff."

"Then you really should get interested in basketball," Val told her. "If we have a good team this year it will be mostly because of Jeff."

Lavina shrugged listlessly. "A lot of good that will do him."

"Of course it will do him good! He'll enjoy it and—and—" she was so indignant she could hardly speak.

"It won't get him anywhere," Lavina said.

Val stared at her. "What do you mean by getting anywhere?"

"Just that it isn't any use. My Mother says we Negroes can't any of us get anywhere in a white world."

"But that isn't true! Lots of Negroes have become successful and famous."

"That's just luck. Kids like Jeff and me don't stand a chance."

"What you're saying isn't sensible. I know your people aren't always treated fairly, but if you don't even *try*, you're beaten before you start."

Again Lavina's shoulders moved in that apathetic shrug. There was no point in continuing the discussion, so Val turned to the matter of Lavina's studies. What was she interested in? Was there any subject that gave her special trouble?

But apparently she was interested in nothing and she had no intention of allowing anything to trouble her. It was a matter of indifference to her whether she passed or flunked, since she was convinced that the end would be the same anyway. All she wanted was to take things as easily and lackadaisically as possible.

"She's just a vegetable," Val told Judy later. "I can't do anything with her."

The minute school was out that afternoon Val hurried down to the gym to catch her father.

"Nick, have you heard? I mean about Tony being appointed sponsor for Jeff Evans?"

Nick looked startled and then a slow smile spread over his face. "Smart move. The more I see of Jeff, the better I like that kid. Tony may have his hands full."

"Except that Jeff does have a temper, even though he seems so gentle," Val pointed out. "Remember how mad he was when Tony didn't want him on the team?"

"Yes, but he got over it just as fast. And he doesn't hold grudges. Maybe this will work out."

"What I want to know is—did you think of anybody I can interview who might work on our side?"

"Sure, I did," Nick said. "You should have thought of him too. What about Jonathan Kincaid?"

"Jonathan Kincaid!" Val repeated the name in dismay.

"Of course. He spoke up at the meeting, didn't he? He wasn't on Millard's side. And you said you wanted somebody important. He's important enough, isn't he?"

"My goodness, yes!" Val said. "President of the school board and owner of the drugstore. But, Nick, I couldn't. I simply couldn't!"

"Why not?"

She didn't want to remind him of that time when she'd been little and Mr. Kincaid had frightened her with his roaring. He'd just think her silly.

"Nick, he barks so. Some of the kids went over to get an interview for the paper last year and he roared at them. I heard about it afterwards. They all said they'd never tackle him again."

Nick was looking at her with those bright blue eyes that always seemed so young. "I thought you were biting off a big hunk when you tackled this idea. Guess maybe it's going to choke you on the first mouthful."

There was no way out. When he talked like that there was nothing to do but go ahead.

"Okay, Nick, I'll see him. But I wish you'd thought of someone else. You didn't have to make it this tough."

He grinned and gave her shoulder a pat. "Go to it, kid. My bets are on you."

CHAPTER 14

INTERVIEW

She walked over to town and went into the drugstore with as firm a step as she could manage. Mr. Kincaid had an office somewhere back of the scenes and she asked a clerk about getting in to see him.

The girl looked dubious, but she disappeared into the inner reaches of the store. After what seemed an endless length of time, she came back.

"Mr. Kincaid will see you, but he's very busy so don't stay long," she warned.

Not any longer than she could help, Val thought grimly. In fact she was ready to leave right now and only the thought of facing Nick and confessing that she hadn't tried, kept her from running out before she went in.

She followed her guide back to Mr. Kincaid's office and was abandoned at the door. As she stood there, looking across the room toward the huge desk and the huge man behind it, the old memory out of her childhood came sweeping back.

Apparently he hadn't stopped booming. His voice made her eardrums ring.

"So! Nick Coleman's little daughter. What can I do for you? Interview for your school paper? I don't like interviews. Always get quoted wrong. Don't like publicity anyway.

There's only one kind of publicity that's any good, my girl. That's what your customers say about you."

She wanted to tell him that she wasn't anybody's *little* daughter and that his customers would probably say he talked too loud, but not being Judy she couldn't blurt such things out in spoken words.

The office was big, like its occupant, and it seemed at least a mile to that huge desk. She managed a few steps before her feet glued themselves to the carpet. It was like marching up to the mouth of a cannon that was sure to go off any minute and blow her to bits.

"This—this isn't an interview," she managed. "I'm here on my own because—oh, because I want to find out about something."

"Well?" he said. "Out with it! Don't stammer. Makes a bad impression on people. What are you staring at?"

What did he think she was staring at? Ridiculously she wanted to say, "Grandmother, what great big eyebrows you have!" Another minute and she'd be crawling back to Nick in complete defeat. In the first quarter of the game. She made the same effort she had made that day she'd played tennis with Tony and managed to look Mr. Kincaid squarely in the eye.

"I was remembering one time when mother brought me into this store when I was about five," she said. "You frightened me terribly. I guess I never got over it."

The bushy eyebrows went up in amazement. "*I* frightened you? Don't be ridiculous. Nobody's afraid of me. That's the trouble. People walk all over me. Come here and sit down, little girl."

Oh, goodness! Val thought. Little girl indeed. Judy was

right about older people. They could certainly be impossible. But it did her good to feel indignant. It stepped up her courage. She walked to the indicated chair and sat down in it, for once remembering her mother's plea not to drop into a chair by just letting go.

"I want to talk to you about the Negro housing project that's opening up in Willow Hill," she said. Her voice wasn't very big, but at least she'd got a sentence out without stammering.

"Well? What about it?"

Val edged forward in her chair. This was where she had to take the plunge, sink or swim.

"I'd like to know what you think of it, Mr. Kincaid."

"Think of it? What should I think of it?"

"I mean what do you think of these people coming here?"

He picked up an oversized paper knife that looked like a saber in his hands and began jabbing at the already perforated blotter before him.

"I believe in live and let live," he said. "If you're after me to side in with this scheme Wayne Millard is cooking up to run the Negroes out of town, the answer is *no*. You're wasting your time and mine."

"Oh, but I'm not!" she cried. "I heard what you said about human values the other night at the meeting. That's why I'm here. We want to find someone to stop Mr. Millard from what he's trying to do."

The bushy eyebrows knotted themselves in a frown. "Mm. A firebrand, huh? Out to start a civil war in your own home town. Is that it?"

"But you said 'live and let live'—and that's not what Mr. Millard and Mrs. Manning want to do."

"Now, wait a minute, young lady!" He made a particularly ferocious jab with the paper knife, but at least she'd grown up in the last few minutes. She was a 'young lady' now. "When I say 'live and let live' I mean exactly that. I'm not going out to stir up anything myself. I was foolish enough to try to speak out the other night, but it didn't get me anywhere. I'm going to mind my own business and let other people mind theirs."

"But somebody has to speak out. If everyone just sits by and—"

He leaned forward and tapped her arm gently with the paper knife. "Nick can be proud of having a girl like you. You've got the right idea about all these things. I used to think like that, too, when I was a kid. Guess maybe I still do. Only I don't try to talk about it so much."

She felt easier with him now, less frightened. But at the same time she was beginning to feel that it was hopeless to try to stir him to any action.

"Somebody has to talk about it," she repeated doggedly.

He shook his head at her almost sadly. "Nobody will listen. They didn't listen to me the other night, did they? It's no good my girl. You'll learn the hard way, too. There's plenty that's wrong in this world, but there isn't much you and I can do about it. So there's no use making ourselves miserable. Better look at the happy things. Keeps you from going crazy."

It hadn't been so long ago that she'd told herself that very thing, Val remembered. But now she didn't want to play ostrich. Trouble like this didn't cure itself just because you stopped looking at it.

"But while you have your back turned so you can look at

something prettier, the other things get worse and worse," she said.

"They do anyway. But don't misunderstand me. I'm doing what I can. I've got a few colored boys working for me right now, delivering and doing odd jobs. I'd like to put some Negro girls in at the fountain and to wait on the booths out in front."

"Why don't you?" Val asked.

He shook his head. "I'd lose customers and my other help would walk out."

"They'd probably come back after they got used to the idea. And maybe you'd get other customers who would admire what you were doing."

His big head continued to move in the negative. "I guess maybe I'm too old to take chances and try experiments. Wayne sort of had me at the meeting the other night when he said his family made up his human values. I guess mine do, too. I've got a couple of sons I want to put through college. You're young—you don't understand that angle yet."

"I don't want to understand it!" she cried fervently. "I don't care how old I get, I want to stick to the things I believe in!"

"Tell me something," he said. "You used the word 'we' a while ago. You said 'we want to find someone to stop Mr. Millard.' Who's in on that 'we'?"

"Just some of us at school," she said. "And Miss Kay and my father."

"That's what I thought. I've been hearing a few things. About Nick putting this Jeff Evans on the team. Wayne's pretty mad about that. And just before you came in Mrs. Manning called me about this angel business. She says the

wrong kind of influence is getting loose over at school and
the board ought to do something."

For a little while she'd forgotten about his being president
of the school board. She listened now in shocked silence.

"Do you see what you may be getting into, my girl? What
if the board decides to take action?"

"But that wouldn't be fair! You couldn't do that!"

He moved his wide shoulders in a shrug. "Lots of things
aren't fair. But it hasn't come to that point yet. I only wanted
to give you a taste of this human values business. Would you
still go ahead on this plan to stir up the town if you knew it
might mean your father's job? Do you think *he* would go
ahead if it meant that? After all, he has a wife and daughter
to think about."

She had no answer for that. She had no answer for anything. This was a more frightening aspect than she had
looked at before. She stood beside Mr. Kincaid's desk.

"Anyway thank you for talking to me," she said in a low
voice.

He harrumphed himself into a more cheerful tone. "Tell
you what," he said, "you stop at the fountain on your way
out and tell Dottie—she's the one in green—that old Uncle
Jon said to fix you up with a fudge sundae. Extra big. On the
house. That'll make you feel better. And you come in and
talk to me again sometime. I like little girls."

She got out of his office as quickly as she could. Judy certainly *was* right about grown-ups. Have a fudge sundae, little
girl. A fudge sundae will make all the world's troubles right.

She was walking past the counter when the big voice
boomed through the store after her. "Hey, Dottie! Give the
young lady a double fudge sundae and make it good."

The smell of chocolate and nuts assailed her. The old fascinating soda fountain smell.

"Don't you speak to people you know any more?" asked the boy on the end stool at the counter. She looked about to see Steve with a tall soda before him. "If a privileged character with a drag doesn't mind sitting next to a member of the common herd—how about parking yourself here?"

He patted a stool and she found herself swinging onto it, still deep in discouragement, but feeling that it would, after all, be a bit foolish to pass up a free fudge sundae.

When the dish was set before her she sat for a moment staring at it, not entirely sure she could swallow a mouthful.

"It's probably not poison," Steve said.

She picked up the spoon. "I oughtn't to eat it. I ought to choke on every mouthful. I must be a very weak character."

"What have you been up to now?" he asked.

She told him between mouthfuls of ice cream and drippy chocolate, and he listened with his usual quiet intentness. Just talking to him helped—getting the words out to someone her own age.

"What can we do?" she pleaded when he had the whole story. "What if they get the school board seriously stirred up?"

"This is America," Steve said. "Nobody can fire a coach for putting a Negro boy on the basketball team. And nobody can fire a principal for trying to work things out in a democratic way."

His words reassured her a little and she felt better when they left the drugstore and started for home. She told him about Lavina Dixon and her failure there. "She blames everything on white people, but she won't get out and push for herself."

Steve seemed to get the picture. "That attitude is enough to hold anybody back. The worst of it is it's being handed to her at home, so she can't get away from it."

"That isn't Mary's attitude," Val said. "But there doesn't seem to be any way to know her. She doesn't want to know me, so what can I do? She's terribly upset because Jeff has been assigned to Tony. Steve, I feel guilty about that. It was my idea. I suggested it to Miss Kay."

"Good for you," Steve said.

"But if it doesn't work it may have all sorts of terrible results. I didn't want it to harm Jeff the way Mary thinks it will. I hoped it would steer Tony onto a different course."

"Maybe it will. All you can do is wait and see. But at least there's a chance of swinging it this way. The other way would never have straightened Tony out."

A horn sounded behind them just then and Val looked around to see Tony's red car at the curb.

"Hi, you two!" he called. "Want a lift home?"

Somehow she didn't especially. She liked walking along talking to Steve. Which was a little surprising, considering that having Tony Millard drive up and offer her a lift would have thrilled her so short a time before.

Tony swung the door open expectantly and she and Steve got into the front seat beside him.

"I was just coming over to see you, Val," Tony said. "I'd have been along sooner, but I had some angelic duties to discharge. How do my wings look?"

He wriggled his shoulder blades mockingly and Val won-

dered uneasily what he'd been up to. But she kept her tone
light when she answered.

"I don't think they're growing as fast they should," she
told him. "But they're really a very pretty blue. You can be
quite proud of them."

He snorted. "Kay is nuts. All this angel business. It'll mean
more trouble—that's all."

"Are you having trouble with Jeff?" She was almost afraid
to put the question.

Tony looked straight ahead through the windshield at the
street before him, but an odd expression had come into his
face.

"No," he said shortly. "No trouble with him." And after
that he was silent.

When they reached the Coleman house and Tony pulled
up to the curb, Steve opened the door on his side and got
out. Before Val could follow him, Tony reached across and
pulled the door shut. As Steve looked around Tony grinned
and waved a hand at him.

"See you later," he called. "I have to talk to Val."

He put the car into gear and pulled away with a flourish,
cheerfully ignoring Val's startled protest.

CHAPTER 15

CHOOSE YOUR PARTNERS

"That wasn't nice," Val said as they turned down the next block. "Steve didn't expect to be dumped like that."

Tony was unabashed. "Steve's okay. He won't care. And I'll get you home in a couple of minutes." He gave her a quick approving glance. "I'm glad your hair isn't red."

"What's Judy been doing now?" Val asked.

Gloom descended on him. "What hasn't she been doing? What a woman! I don't like unmanageable females. And I've never seen one with less sense."

"Judy has plenty of sense," Val came staunchly to her friend's defense. "Just because she happens to disagree with you doesn't mean—"

"Okay, okay. I don't want two of you jumping on me. The point is this. You know the big fall dance is coming up at the Country Club in a few weeks, don't you?"

Val's interest quickened. She knew about the dance, all right, but she hadn't expected it to mean anything to her. Ever since she'd been a freshman she'd had a secret yearning to go to one of those dances. Judy's father belonged to the club, but Nick's earnings did not permit such luxuries as membership in the Country Club.

"Yes," she said quietly, "I know about the dance."

"Then how's about it? Will you go with me?"

There it was—she'd been asked to a Country Club dance by Tony Millard. That was really exciting. Of course she'd love to go! So why wasn't she happy about it? Why wasn't she more excited? She knew one reason—Judy. This would have to be talked over with Judy first or she couldn't accept. Besides, there was the matter of a formal. The girls dressed for those Club dances and she'd never had a formal.

"What's the matter?" Tony asked a bit gruffly. "Am I poison or something?"

She was a little surprised that his feelings were hurt. Tony wasn't usually the sensitive type. He was nice to ask her and she mustn't let him know the surprising lack of enthusiasm she seemed to feel toward the prospect of going with him.

"I'd like to go," she told him. "But I'll have to ask Mother first. May I let you know later?"

"Sure," he said gruffly. "Any time."

He turned around another block and back toward her house, driving in silence. She felt awkward, uncomfortable and a little guilty and to hide her discomfort she tried to talk.

"Tony, do be nice to Jeff Evans. Not just because you need him on the team, but because he seems to be an awfully decent sort."

"He's okay," Tony said. But he wasn't going to talk about it and she knew there was something worrying him.

When they reached the house he let her out of the car with a short, "Be seeing you," and drove away.

A strange car was parked on the driveway. She went slowly up the walk and sat down in the porch swing to think. If there was company inside she didn't want to face them right away. She felt troubled and confused. In a way Tony hadn't seemed any more enthusiastic about asking her to the dance than she was about going with him. Yet he *had* asked her, and he had seemed hurt when she had not accepted quickly.

Tony was a very likable person and they certainly clicked when it came to their interest in sports. She didn't want to hurt him, or seem ungracious about the invitation. She remembered how she had felt walking down the hill with Judy the night Stephen Reid had come. It had seemed thrilling then to be included in plans in which Tony Millard had a part. Now it seemed that way no longer. Why? What had happened to change her?

A hissing sound from the garden caught her attention and she knelt on the swing to look over the rail. Judy's red head poked through the hedge and the hissing had apparently come from that direction. When she saw she had Val's attention, Judy waved a beckoning arm and made shushing gestures at the same time.

Val left the swing and went down the front steps. She wanted to talk to Judy about this invitation from Tony Millard. This time she had to open up the subject directly and find out if Judy had any feelings at all on the matter.

The moment she was within reach, Judy caught her arm and pulled her through the hedge.

"You know what's going on in your house?" she demanded.

Val shook her head. "No—what?"

"Mrs. Manning and Mr. Millard are there. And goodness knows what they're trying to cook up."

"Poor Mother," Val sighed. "She won't stand a chance with the two of them."

"I think they're talking to Nick," Judy said.

Nick? That made it worse. She remembered what Mr. Kincaid had said only a little while ago. He'd asked how Nick would feel about putting a Negro boy on the basketball team if it meant risking his job to do it.

"I thought you'd know all about it," Judy said disgustedly. "But I guess you were out riding around with Tony."

There was her opening and she took it quickly. "I rode around all of two blocks with him. He wanted to ask me something. Judy, let's go where we can talk."

"How about the wall?" Judy said. "If you won't be cold. I'm not."

"I'm not either," Val said and they hurried around the Piper house and out to the crumbly wall in the rear.

How many times as little girls they'd climbed to the top of this wall for a session of confidences and secret-telling. It didn't seem much different now, except that their legs were a bit longer, and the secrets more important.

"So you're going to the Club dance with Tony?" Judy asked when they'd settled down on the wall.

Val looked at her in surprise. "How did you know he'd asked me?"

Judy nodded wisely. "Never mind about that. I know. Are you going?"

"That depends."

"Don't you want to go?" Judy looked astonished.

"I guess so. I've always wanted to go to one of those Club dances and it was nice of Tony to ask me."

Judy was picking bits of stone from the wall and hurling them with unnecessary force downhill toward a flaming sumac bush.

"Judy, you're angry," Val said. "I never meant to cut in. He only likes me because I can play tennis. I don't see why he didn't ask you to the dance. I won't go with him. I'll tell him 'no.' "

"Don't be a goon," Judy told her. "If you turn down an invitation from Tony Millard to the Club dance you haven't any sense at all."

"You mean you don't care if I go with him?"

Judy tossed her red head. "Why should I care? Oh, Tony's a nice guy and all that. But there are plenty more fish in the sea."

"Honestly, don't you care?"

"Not one bit," Judy told her positively. "In fact, I'll probably go to the dance myself."

"Judy, will you? Then it might be fun after all. Who will you go with?"

"I haven't decided," said Judy airily. "What are you going to wear?"

"That," Val sighed, "is the sixty-four dollar question. What can I wear? You know I haven't a long dress. I'll be getting one for graduation, but it wouldn't be sensible to buy another ahead of time, when I'd hardly ever wear it."

"Wear one of mine," Judy offered.

Val laughed. "You're a pal! It would come about to my knees and I'd burst my buttons every time I breathed."

Judy pulled her legs up on the wall and leaned her chin against her knees. "We've got to do something. Maybe your mother will have something old that might do."

"We don't wear the same size," Val said. "Besides, every time I borrow something of hers I rip it, or get spots on it, or lose it. I don't think she'll trust me very quickly again since I lost her yellow jonquils."

"Never mind. I'll think," Judy promised. "We'll work something out. We've got to go to that dance together. Wonder who I can get to take me?"

Judy seemed to be cheering up as she talked and Val felt increasingly relieved. This was going to work out after all.

She began counting off on her fingers. "Well, there's Tom Hazelton. He's always after you to go places. And there's Bill Bronson. And Hank Philips. What about him?"

Judy wrinkled her nose. "Tom is always yipping all over the place like a hound dog. And Bill is clumsy. He spills things. And Hank's worse than Tony when it comes to sports. At least Tony's interesting about it."

They both thought a while, but neither came up with a satisfactory choice.

"If you were in my shoes," Judy mused, "who would you try to get?"

"Stephen Reid," Val said without the slightest hesitation and then looked at Judy in surprise. Going to the dance with Steve had never occurred to her, yet the suggestion had come easily and naturally.

Interest came to life in Judy's eyes. "That's an idea! Why not? Tony and Steve like each other, even though they're so different."

For some reason Val felt an impulse to withdraw her suggestion. An impulse she did not altogether understand.

"I don't know," she said dubiously. "Maybe Steve doesn't dance."

"A guy who's been around as many places as he has?" Judy dismissed the suggestion with scorn. "Of course he

dances. And I like him heaps better than most of the boys
we know. There's something going on inside his head besides basketball and stuff like that."

"Nick says he's pretty good at basketball," Val told her a
little coldly.

Judy lifted her chin from her knees and regarded her
friend with a slightly puzzled air. "You don't care if I get
Steve to take me, do you?"

"Of course not," Val said. "Why should I care?"

"I don't know. Only I wouldn't want to cut in if you—"

"I'm not any more interested in Steve than you are in—
in Tony," Val told her quickly.

They watched each other a moment in silence and then
Judy nodded her red head. "That's fine. Because I'm not
interested in Tony one bit. I don't even like him. So how's
about playing John Alden?"

"What do you mean?"

"Well, I don't like just to barge up to Steve and ask him
to take me to the Club thing. Couldn't you sort of—oh, find
out if he'd like to go? And if he'd be allergic to taking me?"

"Oh, all right," Val said. "Since you've gone shrinking
violet."

She hopped down from the wall and Judy walked back
to the house with her, whispering advice on the way.

"You know—do it casually. Make it sound as if I was doing
it because he's new around here. You know how I mean."

"Sure," Val said. "I know how you mean. I'll do my best."

Debby's voice summoned Judy just then and Val hurried
off toward home. She walked thoughtfully around to the
back of the Coleman house. Since she'd cut out a job for

herself with her promise to Judy, she might as well get it done and behind her.

She found Steve on the terrace, stretched in the hammock with a book propped on his chest.

"I'm sorry Tony rushed me off that way," she said as Steve looked up from his book. "I didn't expect it and I couldn't do anything about it."

He grinned. "I didn't mind."

She seated herself on the edge of one of the terrace chairs. "There's a dance coming up at the Country Club in a few weeks."

He put the book face down on his chest. "Oh? You going?"

"I guess so. If I can beg, borrow, or steal a formal. We—we're trying to work up a foursome. Judy and me and Tony and—would you like to go?"

He sat up and swung his legs out of the hammock. "Sure," he said. "That would be swell."

She knew she wasn't making things clear, so she drew a deep breath and started over. "Tony just asked me to go. His Dad's a member, of course. And so is Mr. Piper. So Judy thought since—well, since you're new in town this might be a good chance for you to get acquainted and—" she allowed her words to taper off without finishing the sentence.

He thought about the idea for a second or two. Then he smiled at her cheerfully. "I'd really like to go. Guess maybe I'll see if I can talk to Judy about it now."

He went off toward the Pipers' and Val watched him go. Somehow the prospect of going to the dance seemed much more interesting if Steve was to be one of the party. But she felt as though the partners had somehow got shuffled the wrong way. Tony ought to be taking Judy and Val ought to be going with Steve. But that wasn't the way it had worked out. Tony apparently wanted to go with her, and Steve seemed perfectly happy to take Judy.

At least she'd done a better job than the original John Alden. Steve hadn't said he'd rather go with her. She started toward the back door, smiling ruefully, but before she reached it, Nick came out and walked past her across the terrace as if he didn't see her. He looked angry and the expression of his mouth was grim and determined.

She ran to him and slipped her hand through his arm. "Nick, what's wrong?"

He patted her hand, but his attention was fixed on the project houses downhill. "I guess this is the pay-off, kid. Millard and this Manning woman are out for blood."

Val waited. Her gaze followed his own toward the bare streets and buildings of the project, as if she might find there some solution for a problem that had become suddenly frightening.

"They want me to take Jeff off the team," he said. "Millard thinks there should be a separate team for Negroes."

"What did you say?" Val asked.

The grim line of his mouth tightened and then relaxed unexpectedly into a grin as he turned to look at her. "I told him I was still coach at Willow High and that I'd run the team my own way as long as I held the job."

Val gave his arm a hard squeeze. "Was he awfully mad?"

"I didn't wait to see. I walked out."

"You're a very reckless father," Val said, "but I'm proud of you. What do you think he'll do? Try to get you fired?"

"He can't do anything very fast. In the meantime we've

got our first game of the season lined up. We're playing
Henderson Heights in two weeks."

"Henderson? Oh, Nick! That's starting out the hard way."

"Best way to start. If we can beat Henderson we're on
our way. Winning an easy game won't turn the trick."

"But the team—it isn't ready—"

"We can't waste time. It's going to get ready," Nick said
determinedly. "How did your interview with Kincaid turn
out? Did you go through with it?"

She nodded. "I went through with it, but it didn't turn
out very well. He wasn't as hard to talk to as I expected, but
he wouldn't do anything. He doesn't want to take any
chances and get people down on him."

"That's bad," Nick said. "The school board's likely to
follow his lead."

"Do you think Mr. Millard will really go to the board with
this?"

"It's possible. But the board may not act at once. And if
we can just swing that Henderson game—"

He paused, listening. They heard the slam of a car door,
heard a car pull out of the driveway. Mrs. Manning and
Mr. Millard were gone.

"What about mother?" Val asked.

Nick shook his head unhappily and she knew that this was
one of the things that worried him.

"I'm going to talk to her," Val said. She did not wait for
him to protest or approve, but went quickly into the house.

Her mother was in the living room, curled up in one corner of the sofa, crying into the crook of her arm like a little
girl. She looked up at Val's step and made futile mopping
gestures at her eyes and her pink nose.

"Oh, how *could* he?" she wailed. "How could he be so awful?"

Val dropped down on the sofa and slipped an arm around her mother's shoulders. "Nick isn't awful. He has to do what he thinks is right."

Mrs. Coleman took the limp handkerchief away from her eyes and stared at her daughter. "Who said Nick was awful? I mean that—that dreadful Mr. Millard!"

Val could hardly believe her ears. "You mean—you're not on their side? Oh, Mother—!"

"I don't know what I mean!" Mrs. Coleman cried. "I only know I'm not going to stand for anyone who tries to talk against Nick like that."

Val gave her mother's shoulders a squeeze. "Good for you. I've been wishing the Colemans could fight on the same side."

"I don't want to fight on any side," her mother protested. "I just want everything to be peaceful the way it used to be."

"It would still be peaceful if it wasn't for what Mrs. Manning and Mr. Millard are trying to do."

Mrs. Coleman looked at her daughter. "I think you've been growing up lately. Somehow you sound older than you used to."

"I hope that's true." Val got up from the sofa. "I'll run upstairs and get you a clean hankie and some powder. You don't want Nick to catch you all weepy. He doesn't like girls who cry."

But she felt a little weepy herself as she went upstairs. Even if her mother had not reached the point where she was ready to fight Mrs. Manning, she was at least standing loyally by her family. And that made everything so much better. The weepy feeling came from a sense of relief.

Not that she was going to cry. Tears, even of relief, didn't get you anywhere. Nick wasn't down there on the terrace dripping tears on the geraniums. Nick was getting ready for a battle. A battle that was going to center around a basketball game at school.

She got a fresh handkerchief from her mother's drawer and picked up a compact. Then she paused to look at the calendar on her mother's desk.

The game was to be played at Willow High on a Friday just two weeks off. The following night, Saturday, was the night of the Country Club dance. What would have happened by the night of the dance? Would it be a gay, happy night? Or would the Willow High team have been defeated? If it had, perhaps she wouldn't want to go to the dance. Not even if it meant dancing some of the time with Stephen Reid.

She remembered that as she'd left Judy she had thought of asking her mother about a dress to wear to the dance. But somehow that was no longer the major problem of the moment. That was something to be worked out later.

She went downstairs with the handkerchief and compact in her hand.

CHAPTER 16

FRACAS IN THE LUNCHROOM

The first issue of the *Wand* was going to press. In the Editorial Room—a large name for so small a room—the desk and spare table were littered with galley sheets. Mary Evans sat at the desk, her head bent above the proof she was reading, her pencil moving now and then as she made corrections.

Judy and Val—free because of a convenient morning study period—were cutting up galleys, pasting dummy, Judy wielding a lavish paste brush and chattering the while.

"You put on too much paste," Val protested. "It makes everything so slippery it won't stick. Mary, we'll need four lines out of the piece about the game with Henderson if it's to fit on the front page."

Mary answered without looking up. "Take out what you can."

Val glanced across the room at the Negro girl. Mary had been difficult to approach ever since the angel business had started. She had not been openly hostile, but she had become more reserved than ever. Yet contrary to her fears Tony had done nothing to hurt Jeff. If anything, it was Tony who was being influenced more than Jeff. Once or twice she had seen Tony and Jeff walking down a corridor, talking and laughing together. Even if the talk was all basketball, they did seem to be getting along all right. And Nick said the team was really clicking.

The days were slipping by and still the school board had taken no action. The angels were working at their roles with interest and vigor and the whole atmosphere of the school seemed to be healthier. Val had worked hard on a piece about what the angels were accomplishing and she was prouder of it than of anything she had ever written. She glowed with pleasure over it even now when it was only in galley form. Not even the fact that it would run unsigned could dampen her satisfaction. But Mary had not thawed, even over that piece. Val got a feeling sometimes that she was only waiting for trouble and that she had no belief in this peace which seemed to have settled over all factions.

Val nibbled her pencil and mumbled to herself. "The part about how Willow High has found a real player in Jeff Evans has to stay in. I won't take a word of it out."

"Maybe that's the very part you ought to cut," Mary said softly. "Maybe that's the thing that will make people stay away from the game. And I suppose you want a good crowd."

"What do you mean *she* wants a good crowd?" Judy slithered paste around and then tried to scrape some of it off with a blotter, making a fine mess. "You and I belong to this school too. And we all ought to be back of that game."

Mary worked on without answering and Val put the article aside. It was better to overlook Mary's words, not challenge them.

"I think I'd rather cut this write-up about the Country Club dance," she said, marking out a line with her pencil. "After all, that's not a school affair."

"But a lot of the kids are going," Judy pointed out. "Especially from the senior class. Dorothy Manning's gang will be there in force—which will be ducky. But there's Steve and me, and Tony and you, and—"

Val scratched out a flowery phrase with unnecessary vigor. "Tony will probably be there, but I don't see how I'm going to make it."

"Oh, Val!" Judy wailed. "But I thought you said your mother okayed everything."

"She said I could go—yes. But what good does that do me if I haven't a dress? I've wracked every single brain I possess and I can't figure out an answer."

She had waited until the next day to tell her mother about the dance. Her mother had not been too sure that she wanted her to go with Tony Millard after what had happened, but she'd eventually decided that his father's words shouldn't be held against Tony. She had been sympathetic, but a new dress seemed impossible just then. Val had accepted Tony's invitation without explaining the problem to him, hoping against hope that some miracle would provide her with a formal before the night of the dance.

"But we've got to find an answer pretty soon," Judy said. "Here we are with the dance a week off—and you with no dress. If you don't go, Tony probably won't either and—"

"What difference will that make?" Val asked. "If you're going with Steve?"

"Oh, none at all," Judy was airy. "It's just that I think it will be more fun if we all go together. If only I weren't so short, and Mother weren't so plump. What about your allowance, Val? Haven't you saved any of it?"

"Sure," Val said. "Six dollars. And where are you going to get a formal for six dollars?"

Mary rustled the papers on her desk and Judy made shushing gestures at Val. Mary was trying to work and they were disturbing her. There was disapproval in the sound of that rustle. But then, Val thought, there was disapproval in nearly every word and gesture Mary made toward them these days.

Suddenly Val laid down her pencil with a decisive thump and went over to perch on the corner of Mary's desk. Mary gave no indication that she knew she was there. Her concentration on her work was complete.

"Mary," Val said, "I think we ought to have a talk. Not about the *Wand*. About us."

Still Mary did not look up. "I don't think there is anything to talk about."

"But there is. You've misunderstood the reason why I asked Miss Kay to appoint Tony as Jeff's angel. You might at least let me explain."

"What is there to explain? You know Tony Millard isn't sincere about wanting to help Jeff."

"Mary, listen to me! When Tony volunteered to be an angel something had to be done about him. He could have thrown all sorts of wrenches into the machinery. He could have started serious trouble. There was only one way to stop him. That was to put him in charge of Jeff. Basketball comes first with Tony. And he knows it will hurt the team if he hurts Jeff."

"He'll find a way," Mary said.

Anger began to rise in Val. "You don't trust us, do you? You're just as intolerant as—as Dorothy Manning!"

This time Mary raised her head. There was anger and resentment in her eyes, but she was better in control of herself than Val and she kept her voice low when she answered.

"Why should I trust you? Why should my people trust anyone with a white skin? What have we ever had from you except injury and injustice?"

"But that's not fair! It's not even true! Your father doesn't feel that way. And I don't think Jeff does either. Your father—"

"I can't be like them." Mary spoke with bitter intensity. "All his life my father has tried to help his own people and to get along with everyone. And where has it got him? Jeff's like him. Jeff's good. He trusts everybody. But he's more of a fighter than Dad. And some day he's going to find out how little it pays to trust people. Somebody like Tony Millard is going to do him in. When that happens it's going to be bad. I don't want to see it happen. I don't want to see him hurt."

In the face of Mary's bitterness Val felt her own anger fading out.

"It's our generation that has to work this out," she said. "And it seems as if the only way to do it is by getting together. But we can't get together unless we trust each other."

The sharp clamor of the bell brought the period to an end and Mary began to gather up her things. Val's words had had no apparent effect on her hostility and she went out of the room without even attempting an answer.

"Wow!" Judy said. "You certainly told her a couple of things."

Val sighed. "It didn't do any good. Before this angel business started she seemed to be thawing a little, trusting us more. But I do believe she thinks we cooked that up just to hurt Jeff."

"Well, let's forget it and go eat," Judy said practically.

But neither girl felt very cheerful as they went down to the lunchroom together. They were silent as they stood in line with their trays. Val was thinking about Mary's obstinacy that was so much like Mrs. Coleman's obstinacy. Nobody wanted to give an inch, and it seemed that if they were to get anywhere everyone concerned had to give a lot of inches.

The lunchroom was more crowded than it used to be, due to the influx of new students. When their trays were loaded Val and Judy carried them to an empty table they finally managed to locate.

At the table next to theirs a party of early eaters was preparing to leave. The girls were gathering together their purses and books, piling their dishes onto trays, preparatory to taking them to the tray stacks. Val glanced up to see Ella Tucker and Lavina Dixon standing back a little way from the table with their trays in their hands, waiting for the other group to leave so they could get the table.

She watched carelessly, thinking of how different Ella and Lavina and Mary were.

Judy gave her arm a sudden nudge and she became aware of a little byplay of drama. Dorothy Manning and a couple of her satellites had also spotted the table the other girls were leaving. Dorothy was laughing and whispering and it was immediately apparent what she meant to do.

The moment the first girls left their chairs, Dorothy and her friends cut in and took possession of the table before

Ella and Lavina could wake up to the fact that their priority was not going to be recognized.

"That was a dirty trick!" Judy whispered hotly. "I'd like to go over and tell that Manning wench a couple of things. Let's call Ella and Lavina over here."

She rose to signal them, but events moved so quickly she had no chance to attract their attention. Good-natured Ella was evidently all for giving up the table peacefully and looking for another place, but Lavina had other ideas.

"We were waiting for this table first," she said and put her tray down beside Dorothy's.

"It's too bad you were so slow," Dorothy told her. "You'd better find another place."

"We were waiting for this first and I guess we'll stay here," Lavina said.

Ella hung back uncertainly. She would be loyal enough not to run out on Lavina, but she wanted no trouble. Lavina put her hand on a chair to pull it out, but Dorothy hooked a foot around the rung. Her face was flushed with anger now.

"We don't want you here!" she shrilled. "Go sit some place with your own kind!"

Lavina shoved her tray onto the table with such violence that it struck Dorothy's tray and sent it sliding off the table's edge with a resounding crash of breaking dishes. All over the lunchroom boys and girls stood up to see what was happening.

Dorothy was wild. She took a step toward Lavina and her hand flew up for a slap.

That was when Judy made a football tackle across the intervening space. She caught Dorothy's upraised hand and

clung to it, while Val, only a second behind her, took Lavina
by the arm and pulled her back out of reach.

The uproar was deafening. Everyone wanted to know
what had happened, and some were already taking sides. For
a moment it looked as if there might be a riot. Then Nick's
whistle shrilled through the room and the familiar command brought quiet out of the rising turmoil.

"Back to your tables," Nick ordered. "Miss Kay will look
after this. Back you go, double quick."

He gave Val and Judy one swift look, but Val knew he was
withholding judgment. However things looked, he wouldn't
take anything for granted till he knew the details. A moment
later Miss Kay had taken charge.

"Come to my office, please," she said quietly, indicating
the little group around Dorothy and Lavina. Val saw that
Mary Evans had joined them and for an instant her eyes met
Mary's. There was increased bitterness in the other girl's
gaze. "You see?" she seemed to be saying. "My people can't
expect fairness from you. This is the way it will always be."

Fortunately there was a side door to the lunchroom, where
they could get out quickly without parading under the concerted and curious regard of the entire room.

Miss Kay seated herself at her desk, looking grave and concerned. The girls grouped themselves before her, with Dorothy Manning and her two friends on one side, then Val and
Judy, and Ella, Lavina and Mary on the other.

"Now then," Miss Kay said, "I'd like to know exactly what
happened."

Dorothy burst into indignant words. "Those two niggers
tried to sit at our table and when we didn't want them there,

that one—" she pointed at Lavina "—pushed my tray on the floor."

"You used a word we don't care for at Willow High," Miss Kay told her quietly. "Suppose you start over and tell your story more courteously."

"*They* weren't courteous!" Dorothy stormed. "Those people don't know how to act decently. They ought to be put in a different school. There's no reason why white people have to put up with—"

"Dorothy!" Miss Kay's tone was sterner than Val had ever heard it. "There will be no more talk like that. If you cannot tell what happened calmly, we'll wait until you've quieted. But let's get one thing clear right away. I want every one of you girls to understand this."

She paused and looked around the silent semi-circle. Then she went on, slowly and firmly.

"I don't know what has happened, or who is at fault. But I want this one thing to be absolutely clear. Apparently there has been a somewhat juvenile and over-emotional disagreement between two girls. It is going to be judged on the basis of a disagreement *between two girls*. Not race or religion, or social status, or anything else come into it. I'm concerned only with being fair and just. Now then—Val, did you see what happened?"

"Yes, Miss Kay," Val said.

"Then suppose you tell me about it."

Val related what had happened. She told her story as honestly as she could, but indignation crept into her voice when she came to the part about how Dorothy Manning and her friends had deliberately tried to take the table away from the two girls who had been waiting for it. It was harder to describe the gesture that had sent Dorothy's tray flying off on the floor. She could not be sure whether or not Lavina had meant to do that, so she told merely what she had seen and gave no opinion. Then she told about the way Dorothy had started to slap Lavina and had been stopped because Judy moved a little faster than she did.

When she had finished Miss Kay looked about the circle again. "Mary, what do you say? Did you see this happpen?"

"I saw it from the beginning," Mary admitted. "It happened just the way Val says it did."

"Did you mean to push Dorothy's tray off the table?" Miss Kay asked Lavina.

The spark of anger which had brought Lavina momentarily out of her apathy had disappeared. She looked sullen again, indifferent.

"What difference does it make if I did or not?" she said. "You're against me anyway."

"Not nearly so much as you are against yourself, Lavina," Miss Kay told her gently. "We are trying to give you an equal chance with every other student in this school. But do you understand what having an equal chance means?"

Lavina looked at the floor.

"It means that you have to work equally as hard as the next fellow in order to earn equal rewards. That's something no one else can do for you. Now will you answer my question, Lavina? Did you mean to push that tray on the floor?"

Lavina shrugged. "I don't know."

"As I see this," Miss Kay said, "there is fault on both sides. Yours was the initial fault, Dorothy, for not playing fair in the matter of tables. You girls had no business cutting in to get a table you could see someone else was waiting for. On

the other hand, Lavina, it would have been better if you had
let the matter go as not being very important. There are
better ways to prove your equality than by being quarrel-
some about it. Certainly, Dorothy, you are mature enough to
know that slapping is out. I'm very glad Judy stopped you.
Have either of you anything you want to say in your own
defense?"

Lavina shook her head.

"It wouldn't do any good," Dorothy said. "This school is
certainly going to the dogs when white people can't get fair
treatment."

Miss Kay merely looked at her and Dorothy's eyes
dropped.

"This matter is too serious to be dismissed lightly," the
principal went on. "I am going to suspend both you girls
from classes until your mothers have come to see me. That is
all for now."

Judy gasped audibly and pinched Val's arm. "Did you
hear that?" she whispered as they went out of the office.
"Miss Kay must have no fear of putting her head in the
lion's mouth if she's willing to make Mrs. Manning come to
talk to her about this."

"It's all she could do," Val said. "But this makes everything even worse than it was before. I don't know what will
happen now."

As they walked along the corridor a touch on her arm
made her look around to find Mary Evans beside her.

"You were fair," Mary said almost grudgingly. "You told
everything just like it happened. You didn't stick up for
Dorothy Manning just because—"

"Did you expect me to?" Val asked in surprise.

"I don't know. I didn't think you'd stand by Lavina. Val—" she hesitated as if she didn't quite know how to go on.

"Yes?" Val prompted.

"I've been thinking about what you said about intolerance. Somehow I never thought about there being two sides to that. Could I see you for a minute this afternoon after school? I'll have something to show you."

"Of course," Val said, a little puzzled. But before she could question the other girl, Mary had slipped away and disappeared around a bend in the corridor.

"Now what's up?" Val wondered aloud.

"I expect you'll find out this afternoon," Judy said impatiently. "Right now I'd like to have another try at lunch. Do you realize, my good woman, that we have had nothing to eat?"

CHAPTER 17

THE QUESTION OF A DRESS

Val and Judy waited by their lockers for Mary when school was out. The corridors were buzzing with talk about the lunchroom fracas and about how Dorothy Manning had been suspended. Dorothy was not too popular, but neither was Lavina. Most of the angels, however, were especially indignant against Dorothy. Dorothy had her followers and sympathizers, too, and it was beginning to look as if this might be the wedge that would split the school into warring factions.

"You see," Tony said, fishing his gym shoes out of his locker. "I told you there'd be trouble. There's not much sense in Kay's saying race didn't have anything to do with it, when it's because of race that it happened."

"It's because of Dorothy's cockeyed angle on race that it happened!" Judy told him indignantly. "If some of us had been waiting for that table, she wouldn't have tried to cut in."

"Okay, squirt," Tony said, giving a lock of Judy's hair a maddening tug before he went off for basketball practice.

Val looked around for Steve, but he had already gone down to the gym. A moment later Mary came out of the division room, a sketch book under her arm.

"Let's go down to the *Wand* room where we can talk," she suggested.

Val and Judy followed her, mystified. Mary put the sketch book down on the desk and opened it without comment to a double page spread of sketches.

The other two bent above the pages curiously. Offhand it looked as if Mary had been drawing paper dolls. Five or six figures of girls adorned the pages, all wearing different dresses, but all looking oddly alike.

Judy glanced from the book to Val and back again. "Why —they're you!" she cried.

"Not a very good likeness, I'm afraid," Mary apologized. "I'm not too good at portraits."

"But they *do* look like me," Val agreed. "Except that their hair-do's are nicer than mine. And they all have long dresses —which I certainly don't have."

"Do you like any of the dresses?" Mary asked. "I tried to design them with you in mind."

"They're not like anything I've ever worn," Val mused. "I think they look better than anything I've ever worn. But why—"

"Perhaps I'd better explain," Mary said quickly. She was almost embarrassed and her usual evenness of manner was lacking. "I heard you and Judy talking this morning about the way you didn't have a dress for the Club dance. But you said you had six dollars, Val, and that would be about enough to buy the material for a dress."

Val looked at her wonderingly. "You mean *make* a dress? But, Mary I've never made a dress in my life. I'm hopeless with a needle. And so is mother."

Mary bent above the parade of fashion mannequins. "I'd

like to make a dress for you, if you'd let me. I'm really pretty good. I make all my own clothes, and I've made things for Linda, too, so it wouldn't be too bad."

Judy let out the first whoop of enthusiasm. "Val! This is the answer! Oh, Mary, you're wonderful. Val, tell her she's wonderful!"

"I'm too stunned," Val said. "Mary, would you really? I've always admired your dresses and wondered where you got them. And I was beginning to think I couldn't go to the dance."

"Tell me which one of the designs you like," Mary said. "I think we're about the same size. I have a pattern at home to use as a foundation and I can manage the rest."

They bent over the drawings together.

"This is sort of cute," Judy said, putting a finger on a girly-girly sort of dress in pale blue.

Mary shook her head. "I drew that one because that's the way Val usually dresses. But I think she ought to stay away from fluffy-ruffles."

"Mother looks so nice in fluffy-ruffles that she always wants me to dress that way," Val said. "This is the one I like."

It was the third drawing and Mary nodded approval.

"I think that would be fine on you. Long, sweeping lines and broad planes of color. You're the vivid brunette type and you ought to play it up."

"My goodness—is that what I am?" Val asked. "And all this time I've never suspected it! You're scaring me a little, Mary."

Mary laughed cheerfully, naturally. She sounded a little like Jeff when she laughed. It was a pleasant sound, and one Judy and Val had never heard from her before.

"Val, let's do this in yellow," she said.

Judy bounced enthusiastically. "You'll be a knockout in yellow, Val. And my dress is green, so we'll go together like a corsage. Why don't you go down and get the material this afternoon? Mary only has a week."

"When could you start, Mary?" Val asked.

"Any time you say. Tomorrow, if you like."

Val nodded. "Tomorrow will be fine. I'll get the material this afternoon and then we'll be set."

"We haven't a sewing machine," Judy said, "or you could come to my place. Where will you work?"

Val answered with an assurance she did not entirely feel. "We have a machine that belonged to an aunt. I'll get it out tonight and see how it looks. Then if you'll come to my house after school tomorrow—"

Mary glanced at her quickly and then away. "Do you think it will be all right—?"

"It will be all right," Val said.

Later, as she went up the steps of the Coleman house, she wondered just how all right it was going to be. Mary knew perfectly well that Mrs. Coleman had been working with Mrs. Manning, but now that she had put her distrust aside she was ready to leave everything to Val.

Mrs. Coleman was in the kitchen baking a cake. Val noted that the operations were nearing the final stage, so she perched herself on a kitchen stool and waited. The minute the batter was in the oven she spread Mary's drawings before her mother.

"I'm going to the dance after all. And this is the dress I'm going to wear."

Her mother looked at the drawings and then at her daughter. "Tell me about it, honey."

"It's my only chance," Val said. "I have enough money to buy some yellow rayon taffeta. One of the girls at school is good at designing and she is going to make the dress for me. May we come over here tomorrow afternoon and use Aunt Sarah's sewing machine?"

"Well," Mrs. Coleman considered the indicated drawing, "I don't know that this would be my choice of a dress—"

"Oh, Mother!" Val broke in. "Don't you see? You've been trying to make me look like you all the time and then we're both disappointed. I'm not cute and pretty and little like you at all. This girl knows a lot about clothes. She makes all her own dresses, and designs them too. She thinks I ought to wear simpler things than I do."

Mrs. Coleman threw up despairing hands. "At least it won't be a very expensive experiment. But don't blame me if the attempt is a failure."

"I won't, Mother," Val promised. "Then I may do it? Judy's waiting for me now to go buy the material. So may I? And may we sew here tomorrow?"

"I suppose so. I know you've set your heart on the dance and I do want you to go. I've been terribly sorry about not being able to buy an extra dress for you just now."

"Then it's all right?" Val urged. "I can go through with it?"

"I suppose so. Who is the girl who is going to make the dress? I didn't know there was a girl in town who could make her own clothes."

"There is. And she makes beautiful clothes. It's Mary Evans, Mother."

By the rush of pink into her mother's cheeks she knew objections were coming, but before she could brace herself against them the telephone rang.

"Why didn't you tell me at once that it was Mary Evans?" her mother demanded. "Wait till I answer the phone. This puts a different light on the entire matter."

Val followed her mother into the hall, waiting impatiently while she lifted the receiver.

"Hello," her mother said. And then, "Oh, yes, Mrs. Manning."

Manning again. And at this particular moment, Val thought desperately. Now what was up?

"Why, how terrible!" Mrs. Coleman said. "You mean there was really a riot?"

Oh, goodness! That meant the lunchroom trouble. She might have known Mrs. Manning wouldn't let much grass grow under her feet over that.

"But I don't understand," her mother went on. "How could it be Val's fault that Dorothy was suspended?"

Val stiffened. So that was to be the angle of attack? No wonder Dorothy was so spoiled and impossible for her mother backed her up in everything she did, right or wrong.

"Just a moment." Her mother put a hand over the mouthpiece and turned to Val. "She's so furious I can't make any sense out of what she's saying. Tell me what happened quickly."

Val told her in as few words as possible. Her mother listened and then turned back to the phone.

"Val is here now, Mrs. Manning. I just asked for her version. And while I agree that these things wouldn't happen if different arrangements were made, I do think Val had to tell the truth as she saw it."

Val could hear the angry sputtering at the other end of the phone. There were tears coming up in her mother's eyes as she listened, but she stood her ground.

"I'm sorry," she said, with an effort at firmness that went off into a slight quaver, "but I can't believe that Val would deliberately falsify in an effort to hurt Dorothy. Whatever story she told Miss Kay must have been what truly happened. If you would just—" but the click of Mrs. Manning hanging up was audible to Val.

Mrs. Coleman put the phone down and the pinkness was bright in her cheeks. "If that woman thinks for one minute that I'll listen to the things she acused you of! I've always thought Dorothy was badly behaved and badly brought up."

Val flung long arms about her mother and hugged her hard. "You stuck up for me! You didn't believe her!"

"Val, don't! You're squashing me. What sort of mother do you think I am?"

"The swellest ever," Val cried. "And don't think I don't know how hard this makes it for you. Now the Colemans are in worse than ever."

"The Colemans are going to stick together," her mother said.

"Then what about the dress? Will you let Mary come over here to make it?"

Mrs. Coleman extricated herself from her daughter's bone-crushing grasp and walked slowly down the hall toward the kitchen. At the door she turned back for a moment.

"I suppose I'll have to let her come," she said. "After all, some Negroes make very good seamstresses."

Val did not stop to argue the point. She ran out to the porch where Judy was waiting in the swing.

"Come along!" she cried. "We've got to get going before she changes her mind."

The purchases that afternoon necessitated a slight indebtedness to Judy on future allowances. But the sunny yellow taffeta looked good enough to eat. Just holding the package in her hands on the way home made some of the ugliness of the day slip away. Mary was nice. It was because of Mary that she could go to the dance. And her mother hadn't allowed Mrs. Manning to thrust the blame for the lunchroom thing where it did not belong. What's more, she was permitting Mary to come to their house the following afternoon. Oh, a lot of things were looking up.

Stephen Reid was coming down the stairs when she entered the house and she waved the package at him triumphantly.

"My dress! I'm going to the dance after all. Mary's going to make it for me."

One of the nicest things about Steve was the way he made you feel that he enjoyed your good fortune as much as he did his own. Tony wouldn't have understood the importance of that dress. Steve understood it perfectly.

"That was swell of Mary," he said. "I'm glad you're going."

There was an especially nice moment when he stood on the stairs looking down at her. Then she caught the parcel against her heart and ran past him up to her room, to toss it on the bed and whirl before her mirror. To her eyes the girl in the glass was wearing a gown of sunny yellow taffeta and somehow she didn't look like the old Val Coleman at all.

She looked like someone different and exciting and—and
vivid. Someone Stephen Reid might like to dance with.

"It's going to be a beautiful evening," she told the girl who
smiled back at her so confidently. "Willow High will have
beaten Henderson. Jeff Evans will be the school's star player.
Nobody can say Nick Coleman isn't a good coach then. Mary
Evans will have made me the most beautiful dress ever."

And—and Stephen Reid—well, Steve was going to like her
in that yellow taffeta gown.

She danced over to her window, moving lightly in the
arms of an imaginary partner. A make-believe orchestra was
playing an old tune, *Just the Way You Look Tonight*. She
hummed the words happily as she looked out the window.
The shadows of late afternoon lay deep on the hillside and
the project houses were touched with a magic golden light.
But not even the gold paint-brush of sunset could make
things down there look gay.

Her dancing partner disappeared like Cinderella's coach.
The lovely orchestra stopped playing and the yellow gown
was only a length of goods in a brown paper parcel.

"What if it doesn't happen like that at all?" she whispered
to herself. "What if I'm just kidding myself and it *can't* happen like that?"

CHAPTER 18

STORM SIGNALS

When Val, Judy and Mary reached the Coleman house after school the next day, they found that Aunt Sarah's sewing machine had been dusted and oiled and set up in state in the dining room.

Mrs. Coleman greeted Mary with the reserved friendliness she might use toward a maid, but Val was too relieved over the fact that she had agreed to allow Mary to come to the house to hope for too much.

The three girls set to work at once. Or at least Mary set to work and the other two waited obediently for whatever small basting and pinning jobs might be handed them—tasks at which they could do no harm. Mary worked with a quick sureness that demonstrated her skill, and Val and Judy beamed with pride when she praised their choice of material. Mrs. Coleman popped in and out of the room every now and then to see how they were doing.

Inevitably their talk turned to the game and to the trouble at school. Lavina's mother had come to talk to Miss Kay and Lavina was back in her classes. But Mrs. Manning had not set foot in a Willow High corridor and Dorothy had not been in attendance all day.

"Oh, dear," Judy said, "how can that woman be like that?

I'll bet she can give with that do-unto-others stuff from a platform, but she's never heard of applying it in real life."

Val glanced at Mary, whose head was bent absorbedly over the sewing machine as the yellow cloth slid beneath slim brown hands.

Ever since Mary had offered to make the dress things had been different between them. Mary's final barrier of reserve had gone down and now they could be three girls together— friendly and natural. But there were still things Val wanted to know and she wondered if Mary would be willing to help clear up her confusion.

"Mary," she began hesitantly, but when Mary looked up and smiled she went on. "Mary, remember that day down in the project when Patty-Lou pushed Debby?"

For just an instant she thought Mary's old reserve would return. The girl stopped smiling, but she nodded "yes."

"I know white people have done lots of things to make Negroes hate them," Val went on. "But what Patty-Lou did wasn't right either. And you let her get away with it. You didn't even scold her. Why not? I'm not criticizing. I only want to understand."

The taffeta moved crisply beneath Mary's fingers for a few minutes before she replied. "I couldn't scold her. You see, I knew why she acted like that."

"I'd like to understand, too," Judy said. "Ever since it happened, Debby thinks all little Negro girls are horrid. I wish she and Patty-Lou could get together sometime and get acquainted."

"I don't mind telling you." Mary's voice was low, but her words came clearly and she kept on with her work as she talked. "Maybe you noticed that my brother Jack's wife is quite light-skinned."

"Linda?" Val asked. "Yes. She's very pretty, too."

"But Jack's dark and so is Patty-Lou. Linda hasn't had to run into some of the things those of us who are dark-skinned have to face. She can go anywhere and no one treats her any differently from anyone else. She has never been turned away from a restaurant because she is a Negro."

Judy looked up from her basting. "You mean you *are* turned away?"

"Let me tell you the story," Mary said. "A few weeks ago Linda wanted to take Patty-Lou into Chicago. She thought she was big enough now really to enjoy the trip. So they made quite a party of it. The most special event was to be luncheon in a very nice restaurant where Linda had been several times before."

Val forgot about the work in her lap and sat listening in troubled silence.

The other girl went on, no emotion in her tone, though you knew what she was feeling beneath her quiet manner.

"Linda and Patty-Lou went early in order to avoid the rush hour and there were lots of tables empty. When the hostess saw Patty-Lou she took them to a place in a corner that wasn't very good, but she didn't make any objections. Linda got Patty-Lou settled and then left her alone while she went to make a phone call. Linda still doesn't know exactly what happened because Patty-Lou couldn't explain clearly. But there was a white woman at a nearby table and—"

"You mean a white woman picked on a little kid like Patty-Lou?" Judy broke in indignantly.

"I guess she made some kind of scene and said unkind

things to the hostess that Patty-Lou heard. Anyway, she and her companion got up and sailed out of the restaurant. Linda met them as she was coming back to her table and the woman fairly snorted as they went by. Patty-Lou was upset and frightened and after that Linda wouldn't stay. She took Patty-Lou by the hand and walked out of the restaurant and out on the street. They went over to the Public Library where colored people are welcome, and they sat down on one of those long marble benches near the stairs."

"That was awful!" Judy cried. "It was cruel."

Mary went on as if she had not heard. "Linda was crying too by then. She couldn't help it. She knew what was ahead of Patty-Lou and how hard it was going to be to tell her that she wasn't like other people.

"Patty-Lou tried to comfort her and she asked what was the matter. Linda told her the white people were the cause of her tears. After a while she stopped crying, but the party was over. They got some candy bars in the station and came back to Willow Hill without any lunch because Linda didn't have the courage to try another place. Patty-Lou still doesn't understand what happened. But she remembered that 'white people' had made her mother cry and spoiled their nice time. So when she saw Debby, who was white and her own size, she suddenly wanted to hurt her because she belonged to the kind of people who had made her mother cry."

Val found there were tears in her own eyes and Judy was sniffing openly. But Mary's eyes were dark with pain and tearless.

"If I can just make Debby understand," Judy said.

"You were right about one thing, Val," Mary added. "Patty-Lou *should* have been scolded. I didn't have the heart to do it. But when I talked to Linda about it later she knew Patty-Lou had to be made to understand that she mustn't blame all white people for what some of them do."

"Just as Debby has to learn that she mustn't blame all Negroes for what Patty-Lou did," Judy said.

The silence after that was long and painful. To break it Val asked about Mary's older brother.

"How is Jack getting along on his newspaper job?"

"He's not there any more," Mary said. "He's working over at the Hubbard Plant."

Val was surprised. "But why? I thought he was so happy about—"

"He was. He never wanted to work at Hubbard. He can do something more than just factory work. But someone turned on the pressure and the editor let him go. I don't think he wanted to. He was pleased with Jack's work. But we suspect that Mr. Millard—"

The air was too charged with emotion, Val decided. In a minute they'd all be weeping on each other's shoulders.

"I'm going to see about cocoa and cookies," she said. "Mary, don't let Judy ruin my dress while I'm gone."

She ran out to the kitchen, got milk from the refrigerator and began to measure it out. It felt good to release her feelings in some sort of action. What had happened to Patty-Lou was bad enough, but the injustice to Jack Evans was even graver.

"What are you doing?" her mother asked putting her head in the door.

"Fixing up a snack," Val said. "Is there any cake left? If not, we'll settle for cookies."

"Has Mary gone?" Mrs. Coleman asked.

"Goodness no. We've heaps of work ahead of us. A little food will help to—"

"But, Val," there was a protest coming up in her mother's voice, and Val swung around, measuring cup in hand.

"Mother, Mary isn't a servant. She isn't even a seamstress."

"Val—"

But she wasn't to be stopped this time. "All I'm asking for is a chance. Mother, come in now and have cocoa with us. If you get to know Mary you'll feel differently. Please. It isn't fair to judge her without knowing her."

Her mother held out her hand. "Give me the cup, Val."

"You mean you won't let me serve—"

There was something a little wistful about her mother's smile. "I mean I'll make the cocoa. The kind you make can't always be drunk."

Val gave up the cup happily. It *did* feel good to have the Colemans together again.

The cocoa was foamy and topped with creamy marshmallows. And there was coconut cake instead of cookies. Val cleared a corner of the dining room table and Mary took time out from her work for refreshments.

The interlude was not altogether successful, but it was a step in the right direction. Her mother, anxious to betray no hint of prejudice, tried to be natural and friendly. Perhaps after a while she would discover that Mary was a girl very much like her own daughter, to be liked or disliked solely on her individual merits.

When the sewing session was over and Mary had gone, Val followed Judy out to the rear terrace, to find Nick and Steve in sober discussion. The two had just come home from late basketball practice and so serious was their mood that they merely glanced at the two girls and then turned back to their talk.

But Val had news she couldn't wait to deliver. She threw a quick look toward the kitchen window to make sure she was not observed by her mother and then burst into words.

"Nick, Mary Evans is making me a dress for the Club dance. She's even designed it for me. Mother let her come here to work and this afternoon I got Mother to come in and have cocoa with us and talk to Mary."

"Good girl," Nick said and the tone of his voice told her how pleased he was. But his eyes were still grave when he turned to Steve again. "How serious do you think this strike threat is? Do you think they'll try it before the Henderson game?"

"Strike!" Judy cried. "A strike where?"

"At school," Steve said. "Haven't you girls heard about it?"

"My goodness, no!" Val was puzzled. "Who is going to strike and about what?"

"You tell them, Steve," Nick said. "You got the story."

"Only pieces of it. Tony was bragging a little. It looks like the Manning-Millard crowd are trying to work through the kids."

"But how can they?" Judy asked. "There are only a handful like Dorothy—not enough to call a strike. I suppose Tony could swing a few his way if he really went to it, but if there's a serious strike won't the Henderson game have to be cancelled?"

"It sure will," Nick said.

Val was caught by an idea. "Then can't we go to work on

Tony over that? I mean the last thing he will want will be
to see the game cancelled."

"That's what I mean," Judy said.

Steve shook his head. "This is worse than you know. It's
not just a few seniors that Dorothy and Tony might influence
who may walk out. If this goes through I suspect it will take
in the entire west side crowd."

Val listened in growing dismay. The greater proportion
of students at the school came from the crowded west side.
Their parents were the small storekeepers of the town, the
clerks and the working men. Some of them commuted to
jobs in Chicago and owned or rented small homes in Willow
Hill. Theirs were not the show places of the town, but they
were certainly its backbone.

"I can see how that would work," Nick said soberly. "Millard has a finger on a good many pay checks. He could drop
a word here and there and papa or mama would come home
and explain to Johnny how a strike might help to get the
Negroes out of the school. And that's bad."

Val had dropped down on an ottoman at her father's side.
She sat with her hands clasped about her knees, her gaze
fixed on distant treetops, as if by looking at something beyond the confines of Willow Hill she might find an answer.

"I don't believe that!" she cried. "I mean I don't believe
the kids in this town are so spineless that they'll let their
parents make them go on strike to get the Negroes out. Why,
some of those west side boys and girls, from freshmen classes
up, have been our best angels."

"But if their parents build it up enough," Steve said, "and
really throw a scare into them—"

"I don't believe Mr. Millard can get everybody in town

fired the way he got Jack Evans fired from the newspaper!"
Val said stormily.

Nick looked at her. "Did he do that?"

"Somebody did. Who else would it be?"

Nick's jaw was getting that square look about it. "If that's
the way this town is going to be run I'd just as soon get out
of it now. But I'm not going to get out without a fight."

Judy applauded enthusiastically. "That's the stuff. Let's
go out and clip 'em one!"

Laughter broke the tension for a moment, then they were
serious again.

"Look," Val said, "if parents can work through the kids
—why can't kids work through their parents, too?"

"That's an idea!" Judy approved. "Parent-education—
that's what we need!"

"Let's call an angel meeting tomorrow," Val said. "Let's
tell them just what's going on in this town and not pull any
punches."

Steve backed her up. "Val's got the right idea. If every kid
in school would go home and get it across that we don't want
to strike, that we don't want to force the Negroes out, that
all we want to do is get along peacefully so everybody will
benefit—"

"Gosh!" Judy said. "You can talk better than Tony's
father. Val, let's make Steve our speaker at the meeting."

"He's elected," Val said.

Nick nodded his approval. "If you can hold off that strike
till after the basketball game, maybe the game will help."

"*If* we win," Judy said.

"We can win unless something unexpected goes wrong."
Nick sounded more grimly determined than Val had ever

heard him. "Jeff and Tony make a combination Henderson won't be able to crack. If we win we'll be showing what the combination of a boy with a brown skin and a boy with a white skin *working together* can accomplish."

Val stood up. "I'm going in and phone Miss Kay for permission to call a meeting tomorrow. Then I'm going to start calling up angels. How's about helping me, Judy?"

"Sure thing." Judy jumped up too, but before they reached the kitchen door Mrs. Coleman opened it.

"Nick," she called, "Jonathan Kincaid is here to see you. He—he wants to talk to you about some action the school board is considering."

Nick got up from his chair. Those square fighting corners Val had seen before were practically sticking out all over him.

"Action against me?" he asked.

Mrs. Coleman shook her head nervously. "No. Anyway not yet. I guess he's trying to get a lot of opinions. Some sort of petition has been made to get rid of Miss Kay as principal of Willow High."

"Get rid of Miss Kay?" Judy echoed in horror.

She and Val looked at each other and then they started with one accord for the kitchen door.

"Come along," Val caught Judy's arm, "we're going to talk to Mr. Kincaid."

The two girls cut in ahead of Nick and brushed past the astonished Mrs. Coleman in their race for the living room.

Mr. Kincaid regarded their breathless entry with pleasure. "Hello, little girls," he boomed.

Val let the insult go. Some people just didn't know any better.

"You can't fire Miss Kay!" she cried. "She's the best principal any school ever had."

Judy rushed into words right after her. "This is America. You can't fire somebody for trying to make democracy work."

Mr. Kincaid was beginning to look more alarmed than pleased. He waved pacifying hands at them as if they'd been two wild kittens who had started to claw him.

"Now, now, children. Don't get so excited. I hope nobody is going to be fired for anything. Certainly no one is going to be dismissed because of her intention to help straighten out the Negro problem in this town."

"Then what—" Val began, but he did not wait to let her get started again.

"It has been brought to the attention of the school board that Miss Kay may have been neglecting her duties as principal. Even to the extent of permitting riots in the lunchroom."

"There wasn't any riot!" Judy cried. "We were right there. Miss Kay smoothed everything out and handled it beautifully."

Mr. Kincaid looked interested. "Indeed? The version I heard was quite different."

"From Dorothy Manning, I suppose," Judy said scornfully. "I hope she stays suspended for good. If anyone ought to be fired—"

"Besides," Val broke in, "isn't there something called 'tenure' in this state that prevents you from just dismissing a teacher?"

Mr. Kincaid backed away from them and sat down. "That is perfectly true. If Miss Kay felt that any charges brought against her were unjustified, she would have an opportunity to defend herself in a civil court. But in the meantime, of course, she would be suspended from her duties as principal."

"But we need her right now!" Judy wailed.

"Ah, there you are, Nick!" A look of relief came into Mr. Kincaid's eyes. "I need rescuing from these two charming young ladies who look as if they'd like to make short work of me."

"Run along, girls," Nick said, but there was a twinkle in his eyes.

"Next time you're downtown come in and tell Dottie you're both to have sodas on the house," Mr. Kincaid called after them.

Val went disgustedly into the hall, with Judy after her. Steve was sitting on the stairs waiting for them.

"Well?" he said.

"Sodas!" Val hissed. "We're to have sodas!"

"Ssh—sh!" Judy cried. "Listen!"

Mr. Kincaid's boom reached them plainly from the living room. "As a matter of fact, Nick, the board is divided as to its decision. Two members would prefer to take no action at this time. The other two want immediate action."

"So yours is the deciding vote?" Nick asked.

"That's right. And so far I don't know how I mean to cast it."

That was all they heard, because at that moment Nick came to close the door. But before it shut upon him he gave the trio in the hall a slow wink. It was not a humorous wink, but a fighting one. It meant they were all in this together and that not one of them had better say "die."

CHAPTER 19

THE ANGELS GATHER

The angels were filing into the downstairs lounge for the after-school meeting. Judy, who had no talent for keeping still, had appointed herself head usher and was seeing to it that everyone found seats.

Miss Kay had suggested that Val act as chairman, since she had had some experience in running club meetings. Val and Steve had taken their places at a small table at the front of the room. Steve had thought it might be a good idea if Mary said a few words and Val had agreed.

Val wished the quivery feeling at the pit of her stomach would go away. It had been there all day and she had scarcely been able to swallow her lunch. All over school rumors had broken out about the strike. Some of the lower class angels had come to Val to tell her that their parents wanted them to quit as sponsors. Quit right away. Val had said, "Wait. Wait till after the meeting."

This was the meeting. If it failed there was a good chance that the greater proportion of the students would go out on strike against the presence of Negroes in the school. That might force the hand of the school board and bring about the suspension of Miss Kay as principal on the grounds of incompetence. If the strike came soon and lasted long enough, the game with Henderson would be cancelled. Val could not overlook the fact that if Miss Kay could be suspended on a trumped-up incompetence charge, the same thing could be done to Nick. That game *had* to be played.

She glanced at Steve. He seemed his usual, controlled and undisturbed self, but she noted that the pencil he held was never still. He had doodled absent-mindedly all over one sheet of paper and was now starting on another.

Of the three, Mary was the only one who was perfectly quiet. This meant more to her than to anyone else in that room, but she had learned long ago to remain in control of her emotions. Once she caught Val's eyes upon her and smiled. In the last few days Mary's outward manner had changed and softened. There seemed less bitterness in her. But if these plans went wrong she might be plunged back into her old state for good.

The room was nearly full now. It was almost time for the meeting to start. Val was to open it and then Judy was to take the floor for a few moments. Judy had requested that she be allowed to speak and Val had agreed a little uneasily. Judy was known all over school as a comedy character. You could count on a laugh every time she opened her mouth, and this was no time for laughing. But Judy had been so earnest about wanting to speak that there was no refusing her.

Tony Millard was one of the last to arrive and Val watched worriedly as he came in. Judy and he were practically at dagger's points these days, but she did her duty as usher and led him to one of the few vacant seats left at the back of the room. For once he made no effort to tease, but followed her to the seat without comment and glumly sat down in it.

Tony, too, had changed in the last day or so. Something was
plainly worrying him. If only this meeting could swing *him*
the right way, Val thought.

With no teachers present to keep order, the din in the
room was terrific. But Miss Kay had said this was their show
and they must run it themselves. Not even the principal
would be present.

Val was about to lift her gavel and pound for order, when
Judy came rushing over in dismay.

"Val," she whispered, "what'll we do? Shall we send him
away, or let him in? Somehow he's heard about the meeting
and he wants to listen to what we say."

"Who?" Val asked. "For goodness' sake, what are you gib-
bering about?"

"Mr. Kincaid! He's out there now. He wants to sit in at
the meeting."

Val leaned across to Steve and Mary. "What do you think
we'd better do? Mr. Kincaid wants to attend the meeting.
But we were going to bar everybody but the kids."

Mary looked grave, but Steve nodded. "We'd better let
him in. Maybe it will do him some good to listen to us."

Judy's eyes snapped. "That's an idea! I'll tell him he'll
have to sit down and be quiet. I'll put him in the back of the
room where he won't be noticed too much."

She bounced away to take Mr. Kincaid in tow. A momen-
tary hush fell over the room as she ushered him in, and then
the buzzing broke out more furiously than ever. Necks were
craned and curious eyes turned his way, but the big man
followed Judy meekly enough to his place and sat himself
down without a single booming remark.

Val knew she couldn't put off the moment of beginning

any longer. She stood behind the table and rapped her gavel
sharply. It took a minute or two to get the room quiet. But
when quiet came it was of the breathless kind, with every
eye fixed upon her. Val had planned her words carefully at
home and had rehearsed them over and over again, but for
a single horrid moment she was afraid she wouldn't be able
to get one of them out. Then she opened her mouth and
surprised herself by sounding much more natural than she
felt.

"We have called this meeting today for a special purpose.
As you all know, there are rumors of a school strike. Some
of us feel that such a strike would not only be the worst
thing which could possibly happen in this school, but it
would also be the worst thing possible for Willow Hill. We
hope this afternoon to figure out a way to stop it."

They listened, still breathlessly attentive. Val turned to
Judy.

"You all know Judy Piper. She has something to say to us
at this time."

Her knees seemed to meet as she sat down. Judy bounced
up in front of the room. There was laughter at once. Everybody expected Judy to be funny. And that was the wrong
note Val had feared.

Judy waved her hands and said "Qui-et!" out of the corner of her mouth. They laughed some more, but gradually
they stilled, waiting for her to go on, waiting to be enter-
tained.

Judy stood on no formality. "Look, kids," she said, "this
isn't my day to clown. There's some serious trouble stirring
up in this town. As Val has told you, we're meeting here
today to see if we can do anything about it. Or if we're just

going to lay down on the job. In a minute Val is going to introduce the speakers, but first we'll have the Pledge to the Flag."

Everyone shuffled to his feet and waited for Judy to lead the Pledge. She did not turn toward the flag, however, but stayed where she was, facing the room.

"I guess most of us could say the Pledge in our sleep if we had to," she told them. "Maybe we do say it in our sleep most of the time. That's why nobody chokes on those trick words. You know what I mean—that stuff about 'liberty and justice for all.' "

They weren't laughing now. They were listening in startled silence. Some of them looked shocked. Whatever else you might make fun of, you didn't behave disrespectfully about the Pledge or the Flag. You could see them wondering what Judy was getting at, a little dismayed by her words, but waiting to see what she meant.

She tossed her red head and the gesture was a challenge. "I think this is one time when we ought to stay awake while we say the Pledge to the Flag. Of course that means that some of you may choke on those words if you say them wide-awake. So I think anybody who doesn't believe in liberty and justice for the other fellow as well as for himself ought to sit down while the rest of us give the Pledge."

Some of them were watching her uneasily now, still a little shocked. Others had caught the drift and delight was coming to life in their eyes. Good old Judy. That was putting the opposition on the spot.

She waited and there was absolute silence in the room. No one sat down. You couldn't have grown up in America and sit down while others pledged the flag.

Judy turned slowly toward the stars against their field of blue, toward the red stripes and the white, and slowly her right hand came up to rest over her heart. There was a lump in Val's throat as she watched. Judy looked so little beside the tall standard that held the flag, but her voice was strong and clear as she led them.

From every corner of the room the solemn words came almost like a prayer. No one could say them this time and not think about what they were saying.

"I pledge allegiance to the flag of the United States of America and to the Republic for which it stands, one nation, indivisible, with liberty and justice for all."

Judy went to her seat and everyone took their places again. The mood of the room was solemn, thoughtful, just what it ought to be, as Val stood up to introduce Steve. Her introduction was brief, but she wanted it to be as impressive as possible. Steve wasn't as widely known as some of the other students were.

She spoke about the work his father had done, about his mother's books—all work which had contributed something toward a better understanding of America and world relations. She ended by telling them how proud Willow High was to have the son of Douglas and Margaret Reid in its senior class.

Apparently her introduction was a success, for Steve got up to a good round of applause. Val glanced at Judy and her friend's red head moved in a barely perceptible nod of approval.

Now the show was all Steve's, but Val had no inclination to relax. No matter how highly recommended Steve came, they'd be a bit suspicious of a newcomer. They were waiting now, watching him with critical attention, ready to swing either way. But if he knew that, there was no detecting the fact in his manner or the tone of his voice.

For a moment she was worried for fear he wouldn't be able to hold their attention. Steve didn't make the kind of first impression Tony did. You couldn't get to know a person like Steve easily. Knowing him took time.

And then, as his voice went on, she began to realize there was something here she had not expected. He stood comfortably, easily, with no nervous movements of his hands, and yet there was an alertness about him that missed no reaction from any corner of the room. And there was an arresting, vibrant quality to his voice that commanded attention.

"A lot of things are being tried in this town," he said. "In fact, almost every experiment possible is being made except one—that of getting along together. If we fail, what can we lose that isn't already lost if we don't try? If we succeed—" he paused and there was something so electric in that wait that the entire room held its breath, hanging on his next words. "If we succeed, we go on the map in a big way. We make something work that ought to work in America, if it can work anywhere."

Judy promptly appointed herself a one-woman claque and burst into applause that the others quickly caught up. Steve waited calmly for the burst of enthusiam to die out.

"Let's save that for later on," he said, "when we know whether or not we really deserve it. Don't think this experiment of trying to get along together will be a pushover. There are those who will want to see us fail. Some of them will be your own parents and that will make it tough."

"I'll say it will!" came a boy's voice from the front row. "My Dad says if I don't go out on strike, maybe he'll lose his job."

There was a mutter of agreement around the room.

"If that's true," Steve said, "somebody's using a pretty unfair weapon over our heads."

This time a girl spoke up. "Whether it's fair or not, we can't go ahead and risk our dads' jobs."

"Look," Steve said, "if every one of us in this room refuses to go out on strike, if all of you go on sponsoring Negro students, as you've all been doing, do you think there's anybody in town strong enough to fire all your fathers? Willow Hill business would collapse and that wouldn't be good for anybody."

You could see them taking that in, thinking about it, weighing it.

"All we have to do is stick together," Steve pushed home his point. "You've been getting along fine with these new students, haven't you? Nobody can touch us if we stick together. We *can* make this work."

He sat down and this time the applause was louder and more enthusiastic than the polite variety which had greeted him when he first stood up.

Val waited until the clapping died down and then introduced Mary Evans. They all knew Mary as editor of the *Wand,* and the upper classmen knew her as a quiet girl who slipped unobtrusively in and out of classes, somehow managing to make top marks in all her studies without any to-do about it.

Today there was a gentleness about Mary that was appealing. A quality like dark velvet, yet with a depth of intensity in it too. Listening to her you knew that she had felt Steve's words more deeply than anyone else.

She spoke simply enough, telling them how much the project meant to the Negroes who were coming to live in the houses. Of the crowded conditions in her own home, and how happy her family was because word had just come that they could move into one of those pleasant new houses.

She told them how much it meant to her brother Jeff to have been accepted on the basketball team, and how hard he meant to work for the team's success in the game with Henderson next Friday.

"Tony Millard has helped him a lot," she said. "Tony has been working with him every day, helping to get his form right."

Necks craned in Tony's direction, but he sat with his gaze fixed on the floor and there was no telling by the straight line of his mouth what his thoughts might be.

Deep sincerity rang in Mary's voice as she went on. "Speaking for Jeff and for the other new students in this school, I want to thank all of you for what you have done in making them feel wanted here, in helping them to fit in. At first some of us didn't believe you really wanted to help. I was one of those. But now we've seen your plan begin to work and we hope you won't let anything stop it."

Her sincerity had won them and she sat down to an outburst of applause. It was time to make a few closing remarks and dismiss the meeting. They quieted as Val stood up.

"Take these things we've discussed this afternoon home to your families and talk them over," she said. "Don't let anybody persuade you to walk out on Willow High. Because if you do, you'll be walking out on your own interests and your own future. You angels aren't the whole school by any means, but you can get busy now and see how many people you can bring over to our side. If *you* stand fast, any effort to strike will look weak and silly. Thank you all for coming."

A rustle and chatter broke out as they started up from their seats, but Tony Millard's voice broke through the stir and they dropped back as he stood up.

"Wait a minute, you guys! This all sounds pretty good in theory. But my Dad says it won't work. He's got Willow Hill's interests at heart just as much as anybody else in town. And he says there'll be trouble at that game with Henderson Friday. Wait and see."

There was no help for it—the meeting had to break up on that ominous note. Tony was popular in the school and there was no minimizing the fact that Wayne Millard's name carried weight. It had been an important name in Willow Hill for too long to be brushed aside in a moment's time.

Steve leaned across the table toward her. "You did a swell job of running the meeting, Val."

Her cheeks glowed with pleasure. She knew Steve wouldn't give praise lightly, but only where it was due. She wanted to thank him and tell him how fine she thought his talk had been, but the right words wouldn't come.

She turned at a touch on her sleeve to find Mr. Kincaid beside her. He had been so quiet there at the back of the room that she had almost forgotten him. Now when he began to boom she didn't mind.

"Thanks for letting me attend your meeting," he said. "It was very enlightening. I'm going to suggest something to Miss Kay that I'd like to see worked into our present P.T.A. After listening to you kids, I don't see why we should have just a parent-teachers association. I think it ought to be a parent-teacher-students group."

Judy had come up and was beaming at him delightedly. "Mr. Kincaid, you're wonderful. I think that's a *real* idea. Sometime I'll buy you a soda."

And Val added, "Then Miss Kay won't be—be—"

"I doubt it," Mr. Kincaid said.

Out of the corner of her eye Val saw Tony slipping out of the room. She left Mr. Kincaid in Judy's tender care and flew after him. He was walking fast, apparently in an effort to get away from anyone who might try to stop him and she did not catch him till he was going out the door.

"Tony," she protested, "why did you have to end the meeting on such a discouraging note?"

He walked on and she had to skip to keep up with his long strides. "Somebody has to be realistic," he said.

"Oh, Tony! You're just being blind and—"

"Thanks," he said shortly, "but maybe I like Willow Hill, too. Maybe a piece of it will be my town. And maybe there won't be much left to live in when you guys get through paddling around in your dream boats."

There was no arguing with him. On this one subject his father had twisted up his thinking until he couldn't see things any other way. But she kept step with him for another half block, trying to find an answer.

"Nick thinks our team has a good chance to beat Henderson. Don't you?"

He didn't answer and she glanced at him curiously. His mouth had that same straight, grim look it had worn when he walked into the meeting, but she sensed confusion behind the look.

"You don't believe everything you've been saying," she told him softly. "I don't think you could have worked so hard with Jeff if you didn't like him."

"He's a good basketball player. That's all."

"Just a basketball player? Not a person?"

Again he let her question go unanswered, but still she would not be shaken off.

"If you go into the game with that kind of spirit you're not going to play good basketball. You either go in to win, or you don't."

He turned upon her almost roughly. "That's not it. Something will happen to spoil the game. You'll see. There'll be Negroes there to see Jeff play—plenty of 'em. Suppose he gets fouled or something? There'll be trouble."

"But Tony, Negro boys have been playing on basketball teams in lots of schools for years. And they get along fine. So why should there be trouble here?"

"Wait and see," he repeated grimly.

"They're not looking for trouble. Are you?"

He brushed her challenge aside. "Dad says we'll never win a game with this set-up. What's more, he says it will be a lot better for the town if we never do."

"You'd better decide whether you're going to listen to him, or listen to Nick!" Val told him sharply.

"Aw, lay off!" Tony cried. And suddenly he left her and cut across the street.

She turned back toward home depressed and discouraged. With Tony in such a state of mind the prospects of winning looked less hopeful. If they didn't win, Jeff might be blamed. And so slight a thing as that might swing the whole school against the Negroes.

What she said to Tony was right. You went into a game to win, or—the startling alternative really hit home—you went into it to lose. What if Wayne Millard talked Tony into going into it to lose?

She remembered the time when she had thought it was lucky that Tony's loyalty to his father didn't fall into opposition with his liking for basketball. Maybe that was what was happening now. And if it was—which loyalty was going to win?

No! She wouldn't consider an alternative like that. Tony wasn't the kind to throw a game.

CHAPTER 20

THE GAME WITH HENDERSON

The game was due to start in half an hour and already the gym was filling up. Val, waiting in the corridor for Judy, saw Mary Evans and waved to her.

"How's Jeff feeling today? Out to win?"

Mary smiled, but there was a tenseness in her expression. "All we hear at home is basketball. Jeff eats it and sleeps it.'

"How does he feel about Tony?"

"Everything seems to be all right, but ever since the angel meeting I've been uneasy."

"Me too," Val admitted. "Well, I've got all my fingers and toes crossed. We've got to make a good showing today."

"I hope we will." Mary started on and then paused. "Don't worry about your dress. I'm going to work on it at home all tomorrow afternoon. I'll have it for you in plenty of time for the dance."

"You're swell," Val told her.

A moment later Judy dashed up breathlessly, waving a green basketball ticket. "I thought I'd never find it! I can't think why I stuck it in my powder compact. Probably so I'd remember where I put it."

They hurried into the gym, to find that the stands around the floor and the lower seats in the balcony were already well filled. Two boys were laying a plank over some chairs to make a bench and by moving quickly Judy and Val were able to get places. It was a bit bouncy sitting on the plank because every time anyone moved it jiggled along its whole length. Anyway, they had ringside seats on the very edge of the floor.

The big gymnasium echoed with noise. The teams were out warming up and basketballs flew in all directions. Big printed signs around the walls reserved sections of seats for each school. Henderson Heights was way down at the other end of the gym and they had the far basket for the first half of the game.

Val watched the Henderson boys anxiously. They appeared to be cut along one pattern more than the Willow High team was—not especially tall, but rather stocky and heavy set. There was one Henderson boy the girls were snickering about because of his cowboy look. Below his maroon shorts his legs bowed as if he had just got off a horse.

"He's not so funny," Judy whispered. "Did you see that basket shot? That guy's good."

Val's attention shifted to the Willow team in their green shorts and jackets. They came all lengths and thicknesses. Tony and Jeff were the tallest, but Jeff lacked Tony's breadth and weight. Steve was shorter than the others, but he was compact and solid. Tony played center, while Jeff and Steve were forwards. The Willow High guards weren't spectacular players, but under Nick's steady drilling they had emerged presentably.

"My goodness!" Judy nudged Val. "Look up there!"

Val looked toward the balcony at the far end of the gym and saw the man in the first row. It was Wayne Millard and at his side sat Jonathan Kincaid. This game *was* rating attention.

A stir out in front of the stands took their attention. Willow High's six girl cheer-leaders had run out on the floor. They all wore white sweaters and green skirts in the Willow High colors, and they were a lively bunch.

> *One, two, three, four,*
> *Three, two, one, four,*
> *Who for, what for?*
> *Who ya gonna yell for—*

Everybody was getting into the spirit now. They followed the girls into a "locomotive" and really hung onto it. Out on the floor the teams paid no attention to the cheering, or to calls from the stands, but kept doggedly on with their basket practice.

Nick came out on the floor, and balcony and stands burst into applause. He said a few words to Tony and Jeff and then went over to talk to the referee. At the score-board Tom Hazelton was getting his tin markers in order, and at the long wooden table across the floor, the time-keeper and score-keeper had just taken their places.

The game would be starting any minute now. Val felt a quiver at the pit of her stomach. Usually the first game of the season wasn't too important, but she had never attended a game more important than this.

Jeff was the only Negro boy on the floor and once or twice she saw Henderson boys look his way, measuring him. The Negro students were all out, and thanks to the energetic work of the angels were spread through the stands and balcony. Miss Kay had suggested the day before that a special effort be made to avoid any look of segregation.

Down at the other end of the gym a boy with "Yell" lettered in maroon across the back of his sweater, and a girl in a short maroon skirt were out leading the Henderson bunch in some very fancy cheer routines. Willow High answered by rising to sing their Loyalty Song, and then things began to happen out on the floor.

The substitutes went to their benches and the referee came out with a ball in one hand, a whistle in the other, his gray slacks and blue and white striped shirt making him stand out sharply from the players. He conferred with the two captains—the usual business of explaining floor rules. The two teams went into last minute huddles and then scattered around the floor. Tony and the Henderson center took their places.

All over the gym the noise rose deafeningly. The ball went up for the tip-off and the whistle shrilled. For a single breath every sound in the gymnasium hushed and then broke into echoing din. The game was on!

Tony won the tip-off and Steve had the ball. He pivoted with his back to the Henderson guard and passed the ball to Tony, who got it to Jeff. Jeff was close to the basket. Up went his arm for a push shot and the ball dropped easily through the hoop to score for Willow High in the first minute of play.

Judy clutched Val's arm and screamed with an extremely healthy pair of lungs.

"Okay," Val said, "stop pounding me. I *knew* we were good!" But she was just as excited as Judy.

However, the Henderson cowboy was good too. Those bowed legs could move like lightning and his stocky body was clever at unexpected dodging and weaving that bewildered his guard. The ball flew down the floor to the Henderson end and a Willow player was called on a foul.

The cowboy stood behind the foul line with the ball between his fingertips while the Willow stands jeered. The referee waved his hands at the crowd. The boy with the ball bounced it once and tossed it smoothly at the basket. A wail went up from the Willow crowd and over at the score board Tom changed the Henderson "0" to "1."

Then the ball was in motion again. When Willow High had it, it moved with a speed Val found it hard to follow. But the Henderson cowboy had a maddening trick of holding it calmly, waiting for one of his men to get free of his guard, not minding at all the booing from the Willow High stands.

Tony and Steve and Jeff were playing real basketball that afternoon, however, and at the end of the first quarter the score stood at 7-3 in Willow High's favor. Jeff had made two baskets and a free throw, and Tony had made one.

The Willow High girls bounced out on the floor again, weaving their arms snake-fashion and swishing their pleated green skirts in time to a cheer of rousing approval.

"We needn't have worried!" Judy told Val gleefully. "Jeff's in the groove and Tony's right with him."

"Don't forget Steve," Val said loyally. "There's nobody on that floor who can beat Steve for speed. That Henderson guard's a lot bigger than he is, but Steve gives him the slip like an eel."

Judy threw her a curious look. "Don't forget you're going to the dance with Tony tomorrow night. I'm the one who's going with Steve."

"Of course," Val said. "I was just giving credit where

credit is due." But she went right on feeling terribly proud of Steve.

The two minutes between quarters were up and the boys were out on the floor again. The Henderson players went doggedly after the ball, fighting to hold it and get to their goal. Just as it left the cowboy's hands for a field throw, a Willow player ran against him, spoiling the shot. The referee held up two fingers and the cowboy made both free throws. The Henderson marker was changed to "5."

"That's two fouls so far on Tony," Judy said worriedly. "He'd better watch it. We don't want to lose him as a player."

Val looked down the gym toward the first row in the balcony where Tony's father sat. Did he seem pleased, or was that only her fearful imagination at work?

But those fouls had been accidental. There was nothing wrong. A moment later Tony had gone down the floor with an amazing dribble, passed the ball in a long shot to Jeff, dodged his guard, got the ball back and redeemed himself in a neat field throw that made the basket.

Everything *was* all right. And Tony was being careful now. No more fouls. Up in the balcony it seemed to Val that Wayne Millard looked less pleased.

"He wants us to lose," she shouted to Judy above the din, nodding her head in Mr. Millard's direction. "He wants this game to hurt Jeff. I know it!"

"It can't hurt Jeff the way he's playing," Judy shouted back. "Looks like the only one who'll be hurt is Tony if he doesn't watch those fouls."

At the end of the half the score was 15-10, with Willow High still in the lead. But it was not a safe lead by any means. This was anybody's game and the teams were well matched.

The players pulled sweatshirts over their wet shoulders and went down to the dressing rooms, while the subs came out on the floor for some warming up. Nick would be down there talking to the team, Val thought. If there was any trouble with Tony, he would clear it up.

Willow High's taste of victory was going to its head. The new students seemed to be as excited about the score as the others and they were bursting with pride over the showing Jeff Evans had made.

Up in the rear rows of the balcony some sort of disturbance had started. A few west side rowdies were getting noisier than the rest.

Judy nudged Val. "Those boys aren't all from school. Some of them are older. That's funny. This isn't an important enough game to bring in outsiders."

The prickle of worry that had died down in Val since the game had got off to such a good start began again. She felt tense and uncomfortable when the players came back on the floor. She saw Tony glance once in the direction of his father.

This time it was the Henderson center who tipped the ball to his own side when the whistle blew. In no time it was down at the Henderson goal and the Willow guards were sweating to get it. Goals had been changed and Val and Judy were in a spot to watch every play.

Henderson scored and as the ball came back to Willow, Tony and Jeff dashed in after the same pass and ended in a collision that took them both to the floor, while Henderson recovered the ball.

That was bad, Val thought anxiously. Which of the two

THE GAME WITH HENDERSON
219

had the pass been intended for? Still, accidents happened in
any game. There was always some bungling. But she noticed
the puzzled look Jeff threw Tony when they got up from
the floor.

Henderson scored again quickly and the markers showed
15-14, with Henderson a single point behind. Again Tony
made a super effort and with Steve's help got the ball back to
the Willow goal. Jeff was over in the clear near the basket,
but Tony appeared not to see him and made the basket on
a risky long shot without his help.

It looked as if something was wrong with the teamwork.
The next time Jeff had the ball in his hands he fumbled and
lost it and the west side gang in the balcony started to boo.
A rustle ran through the Willow High stands as everyone
craned their necks to look at the balcony. The next time Jeff
had the ball Val could sense the change in the crowd. They
weren't all behind him now.

Both teams called time out and there seemed to be some
sort of disagreement on the Willow High team. Tony appeared to be bawling Jeff out and the Negro boy had lost
the look of eager confidence he had worn when he first came
out on the floor.

By the end of the third quarter Henderson led by a score
of three points over Willow High. The Henderson team
seemed tighter in its playing than ever and the boys were
moving a lot faster. There was no holding the ball now. It
was rushed down to the Henderson goal and dropped re-
peatedly into the basket. But the Willow players seemed to
be growing more and more uncertain. Steve made what scor-
ing was done, while Jeff tossed the ball three times toward
the basket and missed.

Then it was the last quarter. Eight more minutes to play. Over across the gym the Henderson cheer-leaders were stamping out a "Red hot team!"

"What's the matter with us?" Judy wailed. "Tony's running wild and Jeff's losing his nerve. Why can't they get together? Steve's the only one out there playing basketball and he can't make a team by himself."

"We aren't behind by much," Val said. "We can still win." But she felt no confidence in her words.

Something uneasy had spread through the gymnasium. In spite of the angels' efforts the white students at Willow High were looking at the Negroes with sidelong, suspicious glances. A girl on the other side of Judy turned to her with a shocked look in her eyes.

"Did you hear what they're saying?"

Val didn't wait for Judy to ask, but leaned across her. "What? What do you mean?"

"They're saying the Negroes don't want us to win. They're trying to get even because of what Tony's father is doing outside. Jeff's losing the game on purpose to get even with Tony Millard."

"That isn't true!" Val cried, but the girl didn't listen.

The excited uproar was increasing. It seemed to Val that the clattering voices came back in doubled volume from the walls and distant ceiling. Sound that had been mere noise before now had a scary sort of undertone.

Judy was pinching her arm practically black and blue. "We've got to win in this last quarter," she kept saying. "We've *got* to win!"

Val saw to her dismay that Jeff Evans looked as he had that day when Tony had refused to come out on the floor and Jeff had thrown the ball down and tried to walk off. Both Tony and Jeff were fighting mad, but she had a frightening suspicion that it was not the Henderson players they were mad at, but each other.

Steve was out there now, talking to Tony earnestly, trying to draw Jeff in, but the Negro boy walked away and his action was conspicuous to everyone who watched.

Then the whistle blew for the last quarter and once more the ball was in play.

If Val had had any doubt in her mind about Tony before, it was gone now. Whether his father liked it or not, Tony was in that game to win. His effort was contagious and Jeff and Steve were kept on their toes. Jeff wasn't playing as brilliantly as he had at the start of the game, but he was doing all right, even if he was mad.

Up went the score for Willow High. 22. 24. Now they were a point ahead of Henderson. 26. Three points ahead of Henderson. The Willow High stands stood up and shrieked. But that Henderson cowboy was a fighter, too, and almost as fast on his feet as Steve. He got the ball the length of the floor and threw for the basket. The ball hesitated on the rim of the hoop for a tantalizing minute and dropped through.

The tin marker on the score board read 26-25, with Willow High leading by a point and four minutes left to play. Between them, Steve and Jeff dribbled the ball back to the Willow goal, where Tony made another basket before Henderson woke up. Again the gym echoed with shrieks.

But Henderson wasn't beaten. A foul by a Willow High player—not Tony this time—gave them a free throw and another point. Then the cowboy got the ball and sent it through the hoop to tie the score at 28-28.

One minute to play. One minute. Steve had the ball. From him it went to Tony, who passed it to Jeff. Then back into Steve's hands for a neat field shot. But in the instant before the ball dropped through the basket the referee blew his whistle.

The Willow High stands screamed with one despairing voice and stood up to see what had happened. Jeff had fouled a Henderson player just as Steve threw the ball. The basket didn't count. Back went the ball to the Henderson foul line and their player made his free throw. Once more the boy with the bowed legs was faster than anyone else on the floor. The ball dropped again through the Henderson basket.

The time-keeper threw his towel out on the floor and the game was over. Henderson had won by three points.

Val and Judy sat on their teetery board and stared at each other, while all around them kids poured out on the floor. The Willow High crowd was raging. Their opinion was plain enough. If it hadn't been for that last minute foul of Jeff's, Willow High would have won on Steve's basket. They were mad clear through. All through the crowd the Negro students were separating from the white, drawing unhappily apart. You could tell by their faces what they were thinking. The loss of the game meant more to them than anyone else, since it meant that resentment would again be turned against them.

Val could sense these things as the crowd moved past. She searched the floor to see if she could locate Nick, but the Willow High team had vanished. The Henderson crowd had broken out on the floor and was weaving a triumphant Conga line down its length. But the anger of Willow High

was not directed so much at Henderson as it was against the
action of one boy on the Willow High team—Jeff Evans.

"Poor Jeff," Val said. "Judy, let's get out of this. I feel
positively sick."

They pushed their way toward the door and Judy whispered on the way. "Val, Jeff was awfully mad at Tony. Do
you suppose he really meant to spoil that point?"

Val stopped stock still and let the throng flow around her.
"Judy Piper, don't you ever say a thing like that again as
long as you live! I don't know what happened. But I won't
believe Jeff *meant* to lose the game!"

Don't get excited," Judy said. "I just wanted to know
what you thought. I don't think he did either. But I'll bet
most of our gang thinks he fouled because he wanted to get
even with Tony Millard."

Val put her chin up in a way she'd seen Nick do. "Then
we've got to convince them he didn't. We can't do anything
till everybody cools off, but later on—"

They had reached the corridor and all around them indignant voices clattered.

"Look," Judy said, "there are Lavina and Ella. They're
trying to get through to us. Come along."

Val followed Judy down the crowded corridor to the two
Negro girls who were caught by the crowd. Ella fairly danced
up and down in excitement, but Lavina was apathetic even
now.

"Everyone's against us," Ella said. "It's so crazy. We
weren't out there playing but everybody's acting as if it was
our fault the game was lost."

"It's worse than that," Lavina said. "But that's what we
have to expect."

"They're going after Jeff," Ella went on quickly. "Is there any way to get him away? Do you suppose your father..."

Val put her hand on the girl's arm. "Who's going after him? The kids may be mad, but they won't do anything. After a while they'll cool off and listen to reason."

"No," Ella said urgently. "Not them. It's that west side crowd that was up in the balcony. We were there. We heard them. They've stirred up the other boys. They're going to lay for Jeff and beat him up. Val, try to stop them!"

CHAPTER 21

MOB SCENE

Val and Judy looked at each other. Then Val caught her friend by the arm. "Come along! We've got to find Nick."

They fought their way against the tide back into the gym, dodging the weaving Conga line to dash across a clear space.

As they reached the head of the stairs that led to the dressing rooms a boy came up, brushed past them and pushed his way out the side door of the gym. It was Tony Millard.

Judy called his name frantically, but if he heard her he gave no sign. Two more boys ran up the stairs toward them —Stephen Reid and Tom Hazelton, who had kept the scoreboard. Like Tony, Steve still wore his playing clothes with a coat flung over them. This in itself was breaking Nick's strict rules.

Val and Judy blocked their way before they could brush past as Tony had.

"Steve!" Val cried. "Wait! Listen to me!"

But Steve was bent on a purpose of his own. "Did Tony go this way? Did you see him?"

"Yes," Val told him. "He went out the side door. But, Steve, listen. Some of the west side crowd are stirring up the

other boys. They're going to gang up on Jeff. Find Nick for
us. Let him know!"

Steve's attention came sharply back to her. Then he turned
to Tom. "Hear that? You better go down and tip Nick off.
I'll catch Tony and get him back here."

Steve started for the door and Judy caught Val by the
arm. "Steve's right! Tony's got to come back and help. Come
on!"

They hurried out the side door after Steve, into the dusk
of late afternoon.

Judy spied their fugitive first. "There he is! Across the
street, getting into his car!"

Tony had turned on the ignition and stepped on the
starter by the time they reached him but Steve didn't stand
ceremony. He opened both doors, and the girls piled into the
back seat while he got into the front seat beside Tony.

Tony didn't look around. "I'm not going your way," he
said gruffly.

"But we're going yours," Steve said. "We've got to talk to
you."

Tony put the car in gear without answering and drew
away from the curb. A crowd of boys and girls were crossing
the street ahead and he sounded the horn impatiently, scattering them out of his way. By the turn he made, Val knew
he was heading for the highway and open country.

"Look," Steve said quietly, "somebody's trying to start a
riot back at school. You can stop them better than anybody
else."

"Let 'em riot," Tony said. "See if I care."

"They're after Jeff. What if he gets hurt? What if he gets
hurt bad?"

Tony didn't answer and Steve tried again. "How about pulling up for a couple of minutes? We can't talk tearing along like this."

Tony didn't stop, but he cut his speed down a little. Val leaned forward in the seat.

"Tony, who're you running away from?"

For a second that got him. "Who says I'm running away? What's there to run away from?"

"Maybe you're trying to run away from the fellow who lost that game this afternoon," Val said. "And I don't mean Jeff."

Judy bounced indignantly in her seat. "If you think it was Tony's fault—! Of course it wasn't. It was Jeff who made that last foul."

The car lost speed suddenly. Tony swung off the road onto the grass shoulder and put on the brakes.

"All right, you guys. Go ahead and say what you want to say. I know you think I didn't play to win."

"Suppose it's this way," Steve said. "Suppose there's some-body in town who wants the game to go badly for Willow High because that will make something happen he thinks ought to happen for the good of the town."

Tony's head came up quickly.

"Wait," Steve said. "You can beat me up afterwards if you don't like what I say. But listen first. I'm not saying this guy isn't sincere. That's the heck of it—when somebody means so darned well in the wrong way. But suppose this guy starts talking to his son who's going to play on the team. He knows this kid. He knows clean basketball comes first with him. So he doesn't do anything clumsy like hinting he should throw the game."

Tony was listening now. Not moving.

"Of course this fellow goes into the game meaning to win. But he's mixed up because of the things his father has been telling him. You've got to have confidence to play your best, and he's had his confidence shaken."

"But he got it back!" Judy cried. "He got it back and did his best."

"He tried to," Steve said. "I'll hand it to him for trying. But suppose his father had pounded it into him that he'd better watch out for what another player on the team might do. Suppose he got to watching this other guy with suspicion, expecting *him* to pull something to throw the game."

"That's what he did," Tony said. "Jeff threw the game."

"Wait a minute. Take a look at this other player. He was in there to play good basketball too. And he went into the game with plenty of confidence. But somewhere along the line he got it that this other guy was watching him, not trusting him. What do you think that did to *his* confidence. He began to get mixed up too and he made a couple of clumsy moves."

"I'll say he did!" Tony agreed.

"So you bawled him out, and that made everything worse. When you stopped believing he could make good, he began to wonder about it himself. You got to know Jeff pretty well the last couple of weeks. What kind of guy do you think he is?"

"He's okay," Tony said in a low voice.

"Do you think he's the kind who'd throw a game on purpose?" Steve asked.

"No," Tony said. "He wouldn't do that. I was shooting off my mouth."

"Then if he didn't lose the game for us—" Steve began, but Judy stopped him.

She slid to her knees on the floor of the car and leaned her arms against the seat back of Tony. Watching her, Val knew there was no doubt at all as to Judy's feelings about Tony, no matter how she had behaved toward him, or what she had said. Just as there was no longer any doubt in her own mind concerning how she felt about Steve.

"You're trying to make it look as if all the blame was on Tony!" Judy cried. "That isn't fair. I don't care what happened, I think Tony—"

But Tony turned around in the seat and put his hand on her arm. His mouth twisted into a crooked sort of grin.

"Hold it, kid. I'm glad to have a redhead on my side for once. But I guess there's something in what Steve's been saying. I did get to know Jeff pretty good the last couple of weeks, and he's okay. That's what sort of hit me—when I began to think maybe dad was right and he was going to pull something in the game."

"Tony," Val broke in, "Jeff's back there now in a jam. Maybe he needs what you can do for him."

Tony's answer came in the form of action. He started the car and swung it around, headed back for town. The dusk had deepened along the road and after a few miles the lights of Willow Hill sprang up.

As they reached town and swung around a corner to head for school the car lights picked up a boy crossing the street.

Steve leaned out the car window. "Hey, Tom!"

Tony pulled up and Tom Hazelton came over to the car.

"What's happened back at school?" Steve asked. "Any trouble?"

"There was going to be, I guess," Tom said. "But I got hold of Nick and warned him and he called the police. They chased everybody out and Nick said he'd see Jeff got home all right. So things are okay now."

Tom went on and Tony drew a deep breath of relief. "Well, I guess things are all right. I'll take you kids home and—"

"What do you say we drop off the girls and cruise around a while?" Steve suggested. "Maybe things are okay and maybe they're not."

"You're not dropping us off!" Judy cried indignantly. "We're coming with you."

The boys offered no argument to that and Tony turned down the next block away from school and headed toward the Negro section. They all kept a sharp outlook, but the streets of Willow Hill seemed as quiet and peaceful as ever. Commuters from Chicago were walking home to their waiting dinners, the evening paper tucked under their arms, smoking as they walked, enjoying the brisk fall evening.

But Val could feel her heart thumping with a quick steady beat as they turned down one street after another like a cruising squad car. Somehow she could not feel that everything was settled yet.

They were nearing the poorer section of town now, not far from where Jeff lived. Ahead a lamp had been broken and the street faded into darkness. Tony turned up his lights and a couple of tall figures darted away to the side, out of range of the lights.

"This is it," Steve said in a low voice. "The whole gang's over there in that vacant lot. Laying for Jeff, probably."

Tony made a turn in the middle of the road and drew up

to the opposite curb, with the headlights pointing back the way they had come, lighting up the sidewalk.

"Got a flashlight?" Steve asked.

Tony took one out of a compartment and opened the car door. "You girls stay here," he said. "You don't belong in this."

Judy started to scramble after him, but Val pulled her back. "It's not going to help if they have to worry about us, too. We'd better stay put till we see what's going to happen."

So they rolled down the car windows and leaned out. As their eyes became accustomed to the hazy dusk, they could see figures grouped in the vacant lot, and the low murmur of voices came to them. It wasn't a pleasant sound. There was a rumble of anger in it.

Tony threw his flashlight on himself and then on Steve to identify them. He was the leader now, and Steve the unknown newcomer.

"What goes on?" Tony asked.

The answer was muffled, but the tone angry. Tony's voice reached the listening girls clearly.

"So you're going to beat him up? So you're going to spoil our chances for winning the next game? What a bunch of saps!"

Tony could talk like that and get away with it. But though they weren't directing their anger at him, you could tell by the rising murmur of voices that he hadn't lessened their feeling toward Jeff.

Another voice came clearly now, though Val couldn't identify the speaker.

"What we need to do is throw a good scare into these Negroes. Show 'em we won't take stuff like that black boy pulled this afternoon. Scare 'em good and clear 'em out of town!"

"It was a dirty game!" somebody else shouted, and the rest added further objections.

"Shut up!" Tony's voice cut like a whip. "You weren't out on that floor today. I was. So suppose you listen to me."

Surprisingly they listened.

"You're sore because we lost a game that was almost in the bag," Tony said. "You're looking for a goat to take it out on. Okay—suppose you start with me."

"We don't want you," a voice called out. "We know you're okay. We want Jeff Evans."

"First you take me," Tony said. "I'm the one who threw that game this afternoon."

Judy's grip on her arm was crushing, but in the tenseness of the moment Val scarcely felt it. Silence greeted Tony's words. A silence heavy with astonishment and disbelief.

"Well?" Tony said. "Come on! What's keeping you? There's only Steve and me. Come on and take it out on us."

But they didn't come. One of the boys who had spoken before raised his voice.

"Whaddaya want to protect that nigger for? You didn't throw that game. Who you trying to kid?"

And then Steve's quiet voice cut through the murmur that began to rise, and again Val felt that electric something that held attention and made people listen to him whether they wanted to or not.

"It makes a difference, doesn't it?" Steve said. "If it was Tony who threw the game, then maybe you don't want so much to beat him up. But if it was Jeff, you do. Why?"

Answers came in a jumble. "Tony's one of us." "Tony

wouldn't play a dirty game." "We don't want Negroes in this town." "That Jeff was trying to get even—"

Steve cut in again on the murmur. "But if Tony *did* throw the game like he says—then you aren't as sore, are you? Maybe you're still plenty mad, but you're not mad enough to beat him up. And I'll tell you why. It's because nobody came in from outside to watch that game and to start whispers about Tony. They didn't care whether Tony won the game or threw it. All they wanted was to see Willow High lose so they could put the blame on Jeff and get saps to fall for it. That's what they were up in the balcony for. To start trouble over Jeff."

Steve paused and this time only a voice or two grumbled objections. He snapped them up quickly.

"Sure you're going to say that isn't true—you guys who were here to do this. You're not from school. How come you showed up today to watch a bunch of kids play a game that doesn't matter?"

There was a shifting among the hazy figures in the lot. The boys from school were pulling apart from the handful of others.

"I'll tell you what threw that game," Steve said. "It wasn't what Tony did, or what Jeff did. It wasn't even what you guys did by turning on Jeff when he began to fumble. It's what loses any scrap—from an election to a war. It happens when people begin to break up and turn against each other and fight among themselves. This town's split up like that now and it's going to be tough for us all till it gets back into one piece again and works for everybody's good."

For all that her attention was centered so tensely on what was going on over there in the growing darkness, Val's ear caught an outside sound. The sound of footsteps coming down the walk. She touched Judy's arm and they peered along the bright avenue thrown by the car's headlights.

Out of the darkness beyond came two figures, emerging from the haze as the light struck them. One was Jeff Evans, the other Nick Coleman.

Judy gasped as they came on slowly into the light, and before Val could stop her she reached over the back seat to throw all her weight against the car horn. The gesture was meant as a warning, but neither Jeff nor Nick hesitated. Blinded by light, they could not know who was in the car, or what that blaring sound meant, but they came on without faltering, and you knew by the way they held themselves —the tall thin Negro boy, and the square stocky man—that they were ready to face together whatever might come.

The group in the lot had swung around at the sound of Judy's alarm and all of them were watching the two who came down the sidewalk.

A voice muttered, "Come on, here's our chance. Let's get that black boy now."

Tony heard the mutter. "Okay, come on! But it won't be soft like you thought. There're four of us you've got to lick this time."

Val had sense enough to reach over and turn off the blazing lights. That would give Nick and Jeff a better chance to see, and not make targets of them.

Nick sized up the situation quickly and his voice barked out of the sudden darkness. "Well! What's this? The flower of Willow Hill sportsmanship, huh? I thought I told you guys to beat it for home. You, Pete and Sam and Dick and

Joe and the rest of you. But it looks like you won't be happy till you get the fight knocked out of you."

It was queer the way the edges of that hazy group in the lot were growing hazier, thinning out.

"My goodness!" Judy whispered. "They're breaking up. They're beating it."

The crisis was over. For a few moments the silence of the fall evening was broken only by rustlings. Then Nick came over and put his head in the car door.

"Good night!" he said as he saw Judy and Val. "Can't you two keep out of the middle of things?"

The girls' laughter had a shaky sound as the reaction of relief set in.

Tony came over and opened the door. "Let's take Jeff home," he said. There was a rough note in his voice that hid what he must be feeling. Maybe this day had hurt Tony more than anyone else.

They drove the few blocks to the Evans house in silence. Jeff tried to say something and ended with an awkward, "Thanks."

But when he got out of the car Tony called, "Hey, Jeff!" and Jeff paused uncertainly, waiting for whatever might come.

"We didn't do so good today," Tony said. "But I guess that was mostly my fault. I think maybe we're going to climb all over 'em in the next game."

Jeff's smile was heart-warming. "I guess maybe we will," he said.

That was all. He turned and walked away and Val saw Mary come running down the stairs to greet him anxiously.

After dinner that night Val and Judy gravitated naturally

to their favorite perch on the wall. It was colder now and they sat huddled in woolly coats and played an old game of counting the stars. Somehow it wasn't easy to talk tonight, and yet each knew there was an important matter that had to be straightened out.

"It's funny," Val said, missing a star in the handle of the dipper and starting her count over again, "nothing is turning out the way I'd hoped, and yet maybe it was better to lose that game than to win it."

Judy smiled at a big rising moon. "Wasn't Tony swell?"

"So was Steve," Val said quickly. "Judy, how did we get our partners so mixed up for the dance tomorrow night? I think Tony wanted to go with you all along? So why did he ask me?"

"You won't be hurt if I tell you?" Judy pleaded.

"Of course not."

"He tried to ask me, but I was so mad at him for the things he'd said about Jeff and—and all that, that I shut him up before he could get it out. I don't blame him a bit for up and showing me what was what by asking you. Then I thought maybe you liked him pretty much and I didn't want your feelings to be hurt. So I pretended I wanted to go with Steve. I thought if I could just get to go, I'd at least be able to dance some with Tony."

"And lately I've been thinking if I could go with Tony, maybe I'd get to have a few dances with Steve," Val said.

They started to laugh then. They clung to each other and laughed until they nearly fell off the wall.

It was Judy who stopped first. She sat up, threw off Val's grasp and sobered completely.

"Look," she said, "we can't waste any more time."

She jumped down from the wall and Val followed her, still a little shaky from laughing.

"Where are you going?" Val asked.

Judy's head tossed in its old purposeful manner. "Where do you suppose? I'm going to get our partners switched for the dance tomorrow night."

CHAPTER 22

FASHION FOR TOMORROW

Val turned slowly before the long mirror in her mother's room. In the glass a vision turned with her. A tall girl in a yellow taffeta frock, with a tiny row of black velvet bows at the gathered bodice, and the same tiny bows ranged at intervals around the hem, showing here and there between the stiff folds. Around her throat was clasped a strand of Mrs. Coleman's best pearls, and somehow the girl in the yellow frock felt assured that this new Val would not break the necklace or lose it.

But perhaps most wonderful of all was her hair. Mary Evans had done that. She had come over after supper with the dress tucked carefully into a huge box and she had stayed to see that every detail was right. At the last minute she'd said, "Val, will you let me fix your hair?"

She had gone to work skillfully with comb and brush and bobbie-pins. No loose-hanging ends, no effort at curls or fluff —just a smooth brushing that brought two soft wings from her forehead, and looped the rest into a neat chignon on the nape of her neck.

"It suits you," her mother said, watching. "You have a real gift for getting people right, Mary."

There was respect in her mother's voice and apparently

she had forgotten all about her first hesitation when her daughter had wanted to bring Mary to the house.

Val turned slowly before the mirror, until Mary called, "Stop!" and ran over to break off a hanging thread.

The doorbell rang before they were through and Mrs. Coleman hurried downstairs to greet Judy and Tony. Val took one more look in the mirror and then drew a deep breath.

"Mary, do you really think I'll do?"

Mary's eyes were bright with pleasure over the result of her efforts. And they were bright with warmth and friendliness too.

"Do!" she cried. "Wait till Steve sees you!"

Val sighed. "Mary, that's the trouble. I mean Judy sailed in and told the boys we were switching partners. She didn't even ask them if they wanted to switch. You know Judy."

Mary nodded, smiling.

"So of course Tony was tickled pink. He wanted to go with Judy all the time. Even that time he asked me to go with him to—to—" but she didn't want to mention the rally, and broke off. "Anyway, every time he's asked me to go anywhere it was just because Judy had made him sore and he wanted to show her she wasn't the only fish in the sea. But I guess she is—for him."

"The way you are for Steve," Mary said.

Val shook her head. "You're nice. But I'm afraid it isn't that way at all. Steve didn't act pleased or anything about the switch. He just accepted it. It was just as if somebody had handed him a carrot by mistake, and then taken it away and given him a cabbage instead. He was just about that excited over it."

"You wait," Mary said wisely.

Val tilted her chin in the way that was characteristic of Nick. "Well, this is it. I'll have to go down. Come on, Mary."

"I'm going first," Mary said. "Give me two minutes and then come downstairs."

She didn't know what Mary meant to do, but she gave her the two minutes. Then she went to the head of the stairs and started down.

Everyone was in the living room, out of sight of the stairs. Everyone except Stephen Reid. Somehow Mary had managed to send him on an errand at the right moment—just to get him out in the hall. As Val started down the stairs Steve saw her and stopped, looking up at her, waiting for her to come down.

If there had been any doubt in her mind concerning her transformation, the expression on Steve's face would have banished it. She put her hand lightly on the banister and came down step by graceful step, with the little black bows dancing against the stiff yellow skirt.

Stephen's eyes told her that she was graceful and pretty and all the other satisfying adjectives there were. They told her he wouldn't care much tonight about dancing with any girl but her.

When she reached the step that was almost level with him he smiled at her. "You sure do make that dress look wonderful," he said.

She managed a trembly sort of smile as she slipped past him and he forgot about his errand and followed her back to the living room.

There her entry was a triumph. Judy, looking cute as anything in her flouncy green, clapped a dramatic hand to her forehead.

"Good night! To think I'd pick Cleopatra for a pal to run around with!"

Everybody laughed and exclaimed and Tony even took his eyes off Judy long enough to tell her she looked pretty swish. She was pleased that he hadn't been able to think up so satisfying a compliment as Steve's.

Perhaps the way Nick and her mother looked was almost the nicest thing of all.

After that, the evening began to slide by in a sort of kaleidoscope design, with the shining colors changing every instant to a pattern still more beautiful.

There was the ride out along the highway to the Club in Tony's car, with a big full moon flooding the night with its glow. There was that agreeable moment in the powder room when the other girls turned to look her over and were quite openly unable to believe their eyes.

And there was the first lovely dance with Stephen Reid. Somehow the sweetness of the evening was almost too much to bear just then and she wished she could live every moment over twice so that none of it could slip away without a full savoring.

But the evening went its way as such evenings do, and there were only a few dances left when the four gathered up their coats and slipped out to the side veranda of the big rambling Club building for a breath of fresh air.

And somehow a solemnness fell upon them. As if they were not quite as young as they had been, as if they could be gay for just so long, and then had to come back to sober reality.

Judy leaned upon the veranda rail and looked off toward

the distant twinkling lights of Willow Hill. "I think things are going to turn out all right in our town," she said.

"Anyway we're over the first hump," Steve agreed.

Val began to check on her fingers. "There won't be any strike. We're going to call an assembly and get a few things straightened out with the whole school, just the way we did at that angel meeting. That *is* working. Nick says not an angel joined that crowd that was after Jeff. And now that Mr. Kincaid's on our side, he won't let the school board do anything till we've had our chance."

"Don't forget we're going to have students in on the P.T.A. stuff," Judy said. "That's a big step."

Even Tony made his contribution. "Wait till we play that return game with Henderson! Of course we've got to lick a few other teams first, but we'll do it."

But Tony couldn't stay solemn for long. Yesterday he had suffered a bit, but by now he had bounced back completely. He began to hum the tune the orchestra was playing and to tap out steps on the tiles of the veranda.

"Come along," he called to Judy. "Let's leave the view to these moon-gazers and get back to that floor."

They scooted in out of the cold and Val and Steve had the night to themselves. Val's thoughts were still intent on the things they had been talking about.

"The trouble is there are so many people you can't ever change," she said. "That girl Lavina is one. She thinks her people should be able to demand that everyone like them. She doesn't get it that she has to *earn* liking just like the next fellow. And then there're people like mother and Tony. They haven't really changed. They've just decided that Mary and Jeff are what they call 'exceptions.' "

"That's something," Steve told her. "Every time they really get to know somebody they add another exception. If it keeps on long enough the collection begins to be so big that they find out it's the people they don't like who are the exceptions."

"But what about Mr. Millard and Mrs. Manning? They don't even have exceptions."

"They're going out of style. Intolerance isn't the fashion we'll be wearing tomorrow."

They were quiet for a while after that. The tune the orchestra was playing drifted out to them and a surprised laugh bubbled to Val's lips. Why, that was the tune of her imaginary orchestra that night she'd stood by her window pretending! Pretending that Val Coleman could be pretty, that she was wearing a beautiful yellow dress, and that she could dance with Stephen Reid while an orchestra played *Just the Way You Look Tonight.*

"We can't waste this dance," Stephen said. "I think the song is about you."

He put his arm about her and they moved together around the big veranda.